THE COLTONS:
COMANCHE BLOOD

*Discover a proud, passionate clan
of men and women who will risk everything
for love, family and honor.*

Grey Colton:
The successful judge aspires to join the State
Supreme Court—not be saddled with a sassy single
mom and her adorable baby that he delivered. But the
Lone Wolf can't deny the laws of nature forever—or
his surprising paternal instincts!

Kelly Madison:
The sweet, spunky attorney always found the
Honorable Grey Colton intimidating, but when
he reveals a tender side, she discovers he's truly
irresistible!

Gloria WhiteBear:
Her shocking secret has been revealed—and has put
her grandchildren in unforeseen danger. But will these
Coltons finally find the peace and happiness they
deserve…?

Dear Reader,

Ring in the holidays with Silhouette Romance! Did you know our books make terrific stocking stuffers? What a wonderful way to remind your friends and family of the power of love!

This month, everyone is in store for some extraspecial goodies. Diana Palmer treats us to her LONG, TALL TEXANS title, *Lionhearted* (#1631), in which the last Hart bachelor ties the knot in time for the holidays. And Sandra Steffen wraps up THE COLTONS series about the secret Comanche branch, with *The Wolf's Surrender* (#1630). Don't miss the grand family reunion to find out how your favorite Coltons are doing!

Then, discover if an orphan's wish for a family—and snow on Christmas—comes true in Cara Colter's heartfelt *Guess Who's Coming for Christmas?* (#1632). Meanwhile, wedding bells are the last thing on school nurse Kate Ryerson's mind—or so she thinks—in Myrna Mackenzie's lively romp, *The Billionaire Borrows a Bride* (#1634).

And don't miss the latest from popular Romance authors Valerie Parv and Donna Clayton. Valerie Parv brings us her mesmerizing tale, *The Marquis and the Mother-To-Be* (#1633), part of THE CARRAMER LEGACY in which Prince Henry's heirs discover the perils of love! And Donna Clayton is full of shocking surprises with *The Doctor's Pregnant Proposal* (#1635), the second in THE THUNDER CLAN series about a family of proud, passionate people.

We promise more exciting new titles in the coming year. Make it your New Year's resolution to read them all!

Happy reading!

Mary-Theresa Hussey

Mary-Theresa Hussey
Senior Editor

Please address questions and book requests to:
Silhouette Reader Service
U.S.: 3010 Walden Ave., P.O. Box 1325, Buffalo, NY 14269
Canadian: P.O. Box 609, Fort Erie, Ont. L2A 5X3

The Wolf's Surrender

SANDRA STEFFEN

SILHOUETTE  Romance®

Published by Silhouette Books

America's Publisher of Contemporary Romance

Special thanks and acknowledgment are given to
Sandra Steffen for her contribution to
THE COLTONS series.

For my fellow writers in this series:
Teresa Southwick, Kasey Michaels, Victoria Pade,
Jackie Merritt and Stella Bagwell.
It doesn't amaze me that we learn from each other.
What amazes me is how much fun we have!

SILHOUETTE BOOKS

RECYCLED PAPER

ISBN 0-373-19630-X

THE WOLF'S SURRENDER

Copyright © 2002 by Harlequin Books S.A.

Visit Silhouette at www.eHarlequin.com

Printed in U.S.A.

Books by Sandra Steffen

SANDRA STEFFEN

Growing up the fourth child of ten, Sandra developed a keen appreciation for laughter and argument. Sandra lives in Michigan with her husband, three of their four sons and a blue-eyed mutt who thinks her name is No-Molly-No. Sandra's book *Child of Her Dreams* won the 1994 National Readers' Choice Award. Several of her titles have appeared on national bestseller lists.

THE COLTONS: COMANCHE BLOOD

George WhiteBear

?
Kay Barkley (d)   m   Theodore Colton (d)   m   Gloria WhiteBear
See *"The Coltons"*

Sally SharpStone (d)   m   Trevor Colton (d)

Thomas Colton   m   Alice Callahan

(2) Bram   m   Jenna Elliot

Ashe

(1) Jared   m   Kerry WindWalker

Logan
Peggy

(3) Willow   m   Tyler Chadwick

(7) Grey   m   Kelly Madison

(5) Billy   m   Eva Ritka

Alisha

(4) Jesse   m   Samantha Cosgrove

(6) Sky   m   Dominic Rodriguez, M.D.

Shane
Seth

LEGEND:
m Married
d Deceased
━ Twins

(1) WHITE DOVE'S PROMISE
by Stella Bagwell *SE #1478 On sale 7/02*

(2) THE COYOTE'S CRY
by Jackie Merritt *SE #1484 On sale 8/02*

(3) WILLOW IN BLOOM
by Victoria Pade *SE #1490 On sale 9/02*

(4) THE RAVEN'S ASSIGNMENT
by Kasey Michaels *SR #1613 On sale 9/02*

(5) A COLTON FAMILY CHRISTMAS
by various authors *On sale 10/02*

(6) SKY FULL OF PROMISE
by Teresa Southwick *SR #1624 On sale 11/02*

(7) THE WOLF'S SURRENDER
by Sandra Steffen *SR #1630 On sale 12/02*

Chapter One

Kelly Madison stood outside her locked car in the parking lot next to the county courthouse, rummaging through her bag for her keys. She found a receipt she'd been looking for and notes and briefs for a case she was working on, but not her car keys.

It was nearing the end of March in Black Arrow, Oklahoma. One never knew what it might bring. Today it had brought rain that had turned to ice, making the streets and sidewalks of this friendly city treacherous, especially for a woman eight months pregnant.

A horn honked on the street out front. An instant later, Kelly heard the high-pitched whir of tires spinning on ice. Metal crunched and more horns honked. Oh, dear, she thought, a fender bender. Transplants to Oklahoma, like Kelly, often joked amongst themselves that folks out here just plain didn't know how to drive in wintry conditions. Officials had been known to close schools and businesses if snow flurries were so much as forecast. Back in the suburbs of

Chicago where she grew up, people didn't let a foot of snow and sub-zero temperatures render them homebound. They just threw on a sweater.

She liked it here, though. She liked the wide-open spaces and the incessant hum of the wind, and the people. She liked the people here most of all. Placing a hand on her round belly, she smiled. She'd been doing that all day. ''Three more weeks, sweetheart, and you'll see what an amazing and interesting place the world is.''

Taking her phone from her bag, Kelly pressed 911 to report the accident, which by now included four more cars. The line was busy. Evidently, everyone in town was calling to report some sort of mishap this afternoon.

Now, where were her keys?

She pulled the hood of her brown trench coat closer to her face. Huddling inside her coat, she blinked through a fine, icy mist, and continued rummaging through her bag. Almost of its own volition, her gaze strayed through the driver's-side window.

Her keys dangled from the ignition. She tried the door, even though she knew it would be futile. It was still locked, just as it had been all day.

Even that didn't dampen her sunny mood. She didn't know why, but she felt like skipping and singing and laughing, all at the same time. She felt invincible, as if she could run a marathon and paint her kitchen, too.

With the mystery of her missing keys solved, she wrapped her happy mood around her, hooked the strap of her bag over her shoulder and carefully made her way back inside the courthouse to search for Albert Redhawk, a dear of a custodian who'd used a coat hanger to unlock her door on more than one occasion before she'd left town nearly seven months ago. The heavy door closed behind her, the sound echoing through the entire first floor of the courthouse. The hundred-year-old lights were on, but the place had a distinctive empty feel. Apparently, the painters and electricians, who were in the final stages of repairing the portion of the structure damaged in a fire during her absence, had all gone home at the first sign of bad weather. The treasurer's office door was closed and locked, as was every other door she tried.

Albert was nowhere to be found, either. It looked as if she was going to get the chance at that marathon after all, or at least the equivalent of one. The mile-long walk to her little house on icy sidewalks would take care and concentration. Experience had taught her it would be fortuitous to visit the ladies' room first.

The baby moved, a glorious feeling if there ever was one. Until the past few weeks, she'd sailed through the entire pregnancy without so much as an ache or pain, or even a hint of morning sickness. Her doctor assured her that a low backache and occasional leg strain was normal for a woman scheduled to deliver in three weeks. Placing one hand on her belly and the other on the ache in the small of her back, she smiled all over again and rounded the corner.

"Oh!" She screeched to a halt mere inches from Grey Colton, the youngest judge in Comanche County.

"Easy." His hands shot out to steady her.

Her smile gone, she slid the strap of her bag back to her shoulder, and took a backward step. "I thought I was the only person left in the building."

"You're close. I think there are three of us. You, me and Albert's here somewhere."

As always, Judge Colton's implacable expression was unnerving.

"Do you know where Albert is?" She swallowed. "Your Honor?"

"My guess is, he's down in the boiler room. Why?"

Something, like displeasure, glittered in his dark brown eyes, causing her to answer quickly. "Oh, it's nothing."

His expression stilled and grew even more serious. Kelly held in a sigh. At thirty-three, Grey Colton's face bore just enough evidence of the Native American lineage of his great-grandfather to set the hearts of the women in his county aflutter. Half the time, his expression of pained tolerance made Kelly seethe. Since she'd recently taken a position with a law firm here in Black Arrow, and therefore couldn't afford to get on his bad side, she nodded politely. "I just have to, er, that is…" She sidestepped him. "Excuse me, Your Honor." Giving him a wide berth, she ducked inside the rest room.

Grey Colton released a deep breath through his nose. It was a reflex action his sister insisted had a lot in common with a buffalo's snort.

He took a dozen steps toward the elevator, stopped, and slowly turned. He strode to the window next, and peered out. Sleet pinged against the glass. Seven vehicles were stopped in a zigzag pattern, blocking traffic on the street out front, as well as at the exit from the parking lot below. Since it didn't look as if he was going anywhere anytime soon anyway, he decided it wouldn't hurt him to walk Kelly Madison out to her car.

Not that she would appreciate it.

She didn't like him.

And that was fine with him. He'd heard she was coming back to Black Arrow. All right, he hadn't been any too happy about it. Something about her got on his nerves. He'd met her in the corridor a few times these past few weeks. Three times to be exact. She'd been courteous—he couldn't fault her for her manners—but nothing more. The truth was, his gaze had a way of settling on her without his permission, and it rankled the hell out of him. Actually, he was thankful that Kelly Madison maintained a cool, diplomatic reserve with him, even though he was well aware that she showered everyone else with her sunny, outgoing, upbeat personality.

She wasn't his type. Thank God. Oh, he didn't have any aversion to her wavy auburn hair and clear green eyes, although there should have been a law against any woman having lips that soft-looking or full. He'd heard she was newly divorced. She was obviously *very* pregnant. If that didn't make her completely unsuitable, she seemed to genuinely believe each and every client she'd ever defended was innocent. Grey didn't like naive women, and he couldn't afford to so much as look at one with any skeletons in her closet. Even in this day and age, an unmarried, pregnant woman would be the kiss of death for a man who aspired to gain a position on the Oklahoma State Supreme Court one day.

He didn't know why *she* didn't like *him*, but the fact remained that she didn't. That didn't mean he

could leave her to her own defenses in the middle of
an ice storm.

He tugged at the collar of his white shirt, wishing
he could loosen the tie and open the top button. He
checked his watch, and waited. The wind had picked
up outside. Inside, the courthouse was silent, eerily
so.

He checked his watch again.

He paced to the far end of the hallway. Jiggling
the loose change in his pocket, he paced back to the
rest-room door. It had been fifteen minutes. What
could she possibly be doing in there?

He had a mother and a younger sister, and while
he didn't pretend to understand what women did with
all their little tubes and vials and lotions, he knew it
could take a hell of a long time. He strode to the far
wall again. He checked his watch again. He listened
again.

He couldn't hear a thing.

He was getting a bad feeling about this. Pacing to
the rest room, he raised his fist and knocked deci-
sively.

Silence.

He knocked again, louder.

More silence.

"Kelly?"

Still, nothing.

"Kelly!" His voice thundered through the courthouse.

At least she answered this time. Her "yes" was
more like the plaintive sound of an injured kitten,
raising the hair on the back of his neck.

"You okay?"

"I...don't think so."

He opened the door far enough to stick his head inside. She was lying on the floor, her face ashen. He threw open the door and rushed inside. "What's wrong?"

She lifted her head weakly. "The baby. I think it's coming."

"You *think* it's coming! Now? Here?" His voice boomed, echoing, causing even him to cringe.

She rolled to her side, as if to try to get up.

"Don't move."

Resting on one elbow, she breathed deeply. "I had a little backache. Just a tiny one, mind you. And then, the next thing I knew, I doubled over. My water broke. The pains haven't stopped for more than twenty or thirty seconds and they last well over a minute and a half. According to my prenatal classes, that means I'm in the final stages of labor." Her voice started to shake. "First babies are supposed to take hours and hours. Days. They're supposed to take days."

She wet her dry lips, those full, ought-to-be-a-law-against-them pink lips. Grey's mouth thinned in irritation. "Okay, you doubled over. You're in the throes of labor. Why the hell didn't you call me?"

She'd closed her eyes, and was breathing strangely. He couldn't take his eyes off her face.

Finally, she said, "I...didn't know...you were... still here." She took several more deep breaths before relaxing. Her eyes opened, and her gaze unerringly met his. "Why *are* you still here?"

"Good question." But he thought it was a good thing he was. A good thing for her. That bad feeling was getting worse.

Grey's great-grandfather, George WhiteBear, claimed

every Comanche man, woman and child had his or her own guardian spirit. The old man had made several journeys in search of his of late. Grey had never felt the need to do the same. George WhiteBear's guide was a coyote. There were no coyotes in the Comanche County Courthouse. Some would say that was a good thing. Grey could have used help in any way, shape or form.

He saw Kelly's phone lying next to her on the floor. Lowering to his haunches, he reached for it. "Why didn't you call 911?"

"I tried, all right? Why are you so grouchy?"

He wasn't grouchy. He was focused.

Maybe he was a little grouchy.

He punched in the three digits. At the first sound of the busy signal, he punched the off button. "The emergency phone system must be down."

"Or overloaded."

"Damn."

"I hear you. And I understand your frustration. But my baby can hear you, too, so would you mind not swearing?"

She pushed herself to a sitting position. He could tell it hurt. Her coat was open. For the first time, he noticed she was wearing a long, moss-green knit dress and sensible leather boots. She placed both hands on her stomach, which seemed to be rock-hard. Her green eyes narrowed, and her face grew even more pale.

Grey didn't know what the hell to do.

He jumped to his feet and paced the small room. Kelly moaned quietly. She was in labor. The pains were close and severe. He started to swear, only to clamp his mouth shut before he'd completed the word. He was judge of Comanche County. He didn't swear. He had when he was younger, but not anymore.

Damn it to hell, what was he going to do?

He stared at his reflection in the mirror. The black-brown eyes staring back at him seemed to narrow and dilate. Strangely, a sense of calm settled over him. It started behind his eyes, moving down to his throat, easing the tense muscles in his shoulders, uncurling the knot in his stomach.

"Can you get up?" he asked. Even his voice sounded calmer.

She swallowed tightly and nodded. The moment she tried to rise, she slumped down again. This time, her groan was agonizing.

He turned on the water and punched the hand soap button. When his hands were clean and relatively dry, he lowered to his haunches again. "I'm going to pick you up. Tell me if I hurt you."

"If you help me to my feet..." Her voice trailed away on a sound that was barely human. "Maybe I can walk."

It wasn't easy to help her to her feet. He didn't know where to put his hands. It seemed he couldn't put them anywhere without brushing the outer edge of her breast or the hard girth of her stomach. He ended up putting an arm around her back. She grasped his other hand. Her grip was strong. She was strong. She proved it by making it to her feet. Once there, she leaned against the counter behind her. "Well. So far so good." Swaying, she took a step. It cost her.

Without conscious thought, Grey swung her into his arms. He staggered backward a step. She was slender, but she was about five feet six. And pregnant.

A glance at her face showed a small smile. While she steadied herself by wrapping an arm around his neck, probably in an effort to hold on for dear life, he redistributed her weight more evenly in his arms.

"Are you sure you can do this?" she asked quietly.

The sound he made had a lot in common with a snort again. "Just open the door."

"Yes, Your Honor."

She pulled on the door. Using his foot, he pushed it to the wall, then shouldered his way through.

"Where are we going?"

Until he saw the elevator door that was standing open, he hadn't known. Entering the small compartment, he said, "There's a sofa in my chambers."

He figured she would have argued, if another pain hadn't ripped through her. She squeezed her eyes shut, and he swore every muscle in her entire body tensed.

They reached his chambers before her pain subsided.

This was bad. He had no knowledge of medicine. He hadn't so much as had a cold in twenty years. And while he'd helped his cousin, Bram, deliver one of Bram's prize quarter-horse colts a few years ago, Grey had no idea how to deliver a human baby.

With painstaking care, he lowered Kelly to the leather sofa. Instantly, he grabbed the phone on his desk and tried 911 again. The results were the same. He dialed his mother's number next. He got her machine. He was in the middle of dialing his sister's number when the phone went dead.

Reluctantly, he hung it up.

"What's wrong?" she asked.

"The ice must have taken down the phone lines."

"My cell phone isn't working, either. I'm going to have my baby here, aren't I?" There was hysteria in her voice.

"I think so."

She gasped, and he said, "I can think of worse places." He could think of better ones, too. Hospitals. Clinics. The moon.

Kelly took a series of deep breaths. "The labor instructor lied. Breathing doesn't help."

"It's got to be better than the alternative."

Her pain subsided long enough to appreciate his stab at wry humor. She eased back on the supple leather sofa, taking stock of her situation. The baby was coming. She could feel it pressing lower and lower. It hurt so bad. She couldn't call the hospital or her doctor. But she was warm and dry. And she wasn't alone.

She placed a hand on her swollen abdomen.

"Lie back and rest."

She could hear Grey fluffing a pillow. A moment later, he tucked it under her head.

"Talk to me," she whispered, her eyes closed. When he made no sound, she realized he probably didn't know what to say. She whispered, "Who decorated your chambers?"

"My sister, my mother and my grandmother. Does it show?"

She smiled, again the epitome of diplomacy. "My grandmother made this pillow for me before she died," he said. "She made one for my sister, my brothers, and all our cousins."

Kelly felt him taking the pins from her hair. She focused on the heat in his fingertips. She lost her concentration during the next pain, but he was still there those interminable minutes later, when the contraction subsided.

"What do you say we get you out of your boots?"

She reached for her ankle, but he took over, sliding the right boot off easily. She didn't know whether to be embarrassed or scared out of her wits. Placing a hand on her belly, she thought about the baby and said, "I can do this." She said it six times in all.

The next thing she knew, her other boot was off, too. While he placed it against the wall with the first one, Kelly said, "Women used to have babies at home all the time. We've all heard stories of women who gave birth, then went back to work in the rice paddy."

"It's not quite as bad as that," he answered.

"Exactly."

She brought her legs up, and groaned.

Grey raked his fingers through his hair. "You're going to have to remove some clothes, Kelly."

Her eyes were round all of a sudden. She swallowed her panic admirably. "Would you mind turning around?"

He stared at her for a moment before giving her the privacy she'd requested. "Giving birth is no time for modesty."

"I know, but the only people who are supposed to see a woman like this are her doctors and her lover."

Grey had no business thinking what he was thinking at a time like this. It was the way she'd said lover.

The quiet rustle of fabric on leather was punctuated by an occasional catch in her breathing. "What was your grandmother's name?"

Grey didn't comprehend the question. "What grandmother?"

"The one who made you and all her grandchildren a pillow like this one?"

He turned around again, and saw that Kelly was covered up with her coat. She was still wearing her green dress, but her undergarments were folded neatly on the floor near the couch.

"Her name was Gloria WhiteBear Colton. Her husband, my grandfather, died before she gave birth to twin sons, my father, Tom, and my Uncle Trevor, who died a long time ago. My grandmother raised my five cousins, but she had a hand in raising my brothers, sister and I, too."

Kelly gripped his hand as another pain gripped her. Grey tried to decide what he should be doing. In the movies, somebody always boiled water at times like these. That was the extent of Grey's medical training. He wet some paper towels at the small sink in his lavatory, then smoothed them across her face. "Did your prenatal classes prepare you for what's going to happen?" he asked.

"More or less." Her eyes were closed, her breathing deep and even. "You should have heard me proclaiming how I was going to have my child naturally. What I wouldn't do for an epidural or some other painkilling drugs right now."

"You have your sense of humor. That's good."

Another pain took her. When it was over, she said, "Keep talking. Even when I don't seem to be listening."

"I'm not much of a talker."

"Oh."

"It's one of the downfalls of growing up in a large family. It isn't easy to get a word in edgewise."

"I have one older sister. It was never easy to get

a word in edgewise in our house, either.'' There were a few seconds of silence. And then she asked, ''How many brothers and sisters do you have?''

He ended up naming and describing all four of his brothers, his sister, as well as his five cousins. He wasn't sure she heard half of what he said, but it didn't matter. He sat on a straight-backed chair pulled close to the leather sofa. His chambers were in the interior portion of the old courthouse, which meant there were no windows. The only light came from hundred-year-old fixtures on the paneled walls and a lamp he'd turned on on his big, mahogany desk.

He reminisced about simpler times, and what it was like growing up in a loud, boisterous family. She was breathing quietly when he started to tell the story of the time he, Billy, Jesse, Sky and their cousin Willow had been visiting the family ranch.

''We climbed up a rickety ladder nailed to the wall in the barn. At the top was a window with no glass where barn swallows and doves roosted. From there it was an easy climb out onto the roof of a lean-to that housed straw and machinery and little animals that scuttled, heard but rarely seen. We all knew that roof was forbidden territory. That was half the allure. The other half was the view. We sat up there in a row, smugly enjoying our adventure. Our grandmother's voice carried around to the back of the barn, calling us in for lunch. Being the oldest, I went last, the others climbing down ahead of me. We could smell the homemade soup and fresh-baked bread before we reached the house.''

''What kind of soup?'' Kelly asked.

So she *was* listening. ''Vegetable beef. My mother was stirring it on the stove when we got there. My grandmother, who had been raising my cousins ever since their parents died a few years earlier, looked at each of us in turn. Tossing her gray braid over her shoulder, she said, 'Willow, would you like your spanking now or later?'

"All five of us froze like antelope trapped in the glare of headlights. How could she have known? My ever-wise grandmother nudged my mother and said, 'Are you going to line yours up for spankings, too, Alice?'"

"Not exactly good appetizer talk, huh?" Kelly whispered.

Grey shook his head at the memory. "My mother said that she would prefer to wait until our father got home." He leaned ahead in his chair, quietly adding, "And you're right. None of us ate much at lunch that day."

"Did your father spank you when he got home?"

"I don't think my mother ever told him. I doubt she'd planned to. That six-hour wait was our punishment."

Kelly grew silent, panting through another pain. It lasted almost two minutes. Deep lines cut into the corners of her mouth; her face was wet with perspiration long before the contraction was over. Exhausted, she slumped back. Without opening her eyes, she said, "Do you believe in spanking children?"

"Most of the time, no."

"But?" she whispered.

"If they climb out onto a rotting roof forty feet off the ground, when one wrong move could get them killed, or worse, then, yeah, I believe in spankings. Not beatings, or whippings, but a swat on the seat of their pants, or the threat of one, was very effective."

Kelly thought about that. Grey's mother sounded like a wise woman. The "wait for your father to get home" ploy had worked, probably because she hadn't overused it. Kelly's baby wasn't going to have a father. It was all up to her. She didn't want to think about that right now.

"Tell me more. About that big family of yours."

Grey Colton, a man who'd professed that he wasn't much of a talker, told her about the years his family had moved around while his father had been in the army. He talked about his great-grandfather George WhiteBear and his spirit quests. Sometimes she whimpered. Sometimes she squeezed his hand so hard he feared for the internal integrity of several of his bones. She never screamed or yelled, and by God, he wasn't about to.

Before long, there was no time between pains. Her body strained as if being guided by inner wisdom fueled by some ancient knowledge.

Grey went on automatic pilot. Since he had no blankets or sheets or towels, he removed his white dress shirt and the cotton T-shirt underneath, for later use. The sounds Kelly made now were guttural, her breathing labored as he reassured her and told her she was doing great. A nearly bald head crowned. Soon, a shoulder emerged. He didn't know where Kelly found the strength to keep pushing. She was so tired, and God, the pain...

But she pushed again, and an unbelievably tiny child was born into Grey's hands. "I've got her."

"Her?"

"It's a girl." His throat closed up tight.

The child was warm and moving. Using his T-shirt,

he cleaned the baby off as best he could. It caused her to start to cry.

"What's wrong?" Kelly whispered.

"Nothing that I can see. I don't think she likes to have her face washed."

That tiny, mewling cry grew stronger as he wrapped her in his starched white shirt. Carefully, he placed the tiny bundle in Kelly's shaking arms. The baby stopped crying.

And Kelly started.

She hadn't shed a tear through the entire ordeal. Now she cried, big, fat tears rolling down her face. "She's beautiful."

The baby was bald, wrinkled and red. She needed a bath. "Not just beautiful," Grey whispered. "She's perfect."

Kelly sniffled. "I need to call my mother."

Grey handed her the cell phone. She pushed speed dial, and, lo and behold, the phone worked. She told her mother all about the birth. Of course her mother freaked and insisted Kelly hang up and call 911 immediately.

And miraculously, this time that worked, too.

Grey took the phone from her. "This is Judge Grey Colton. I'm in my chambers on the second floor of the courthouse, with Kelly Madison. She's just had her baby. We need an ambulance and some paramedics up here, *now*. I'll stay on the line. Try to disconnect me and I'll see you in court."

Feeling her eyes on him, he glanced at her.

"Even without your shirt, you're formidable."

She wavered him a woman-soft smile that went straight to his head. He barely managed to hold the phone to his ear.

"Was it worth it?" she whispered.

At first he thought she was referring to delivering her daughter. But then she said, "Was climbing onto that barn roof worth it?"

A lump came and went in his throat. "I can still remember the view."

"That's what I thought."

She pressed her lips to her daughter's cheek. "Why is it that the most worthwhile things in life always come with the greatest risk?"

Their gazes locked, and something nearly tangible passed between them. She leaned back and closed her eyes, drawing the baby closer.

He wished he had a blanket to cover her and the infant. Those paramedics had better hurry up and get here. "Yes." He spoke into the phone. "I'm still here. Yes." He answered a few questions, gave a few details, which he followed up with one succinct order to hurry.

"Help is on the way," he said.

He looked at Kelly. She and the baby were both asleep.

Chapter Two

"Judge?"

Grey looked at the paramedic standing at the front of Kelly's gurney. The man looked back at him expectantly, prompting Grey to reply curtly. "What is it?"

"You need to move to one side so we can get the patients loaded into the ambulance."

Grey got out of the way.

The icy drizzle had stopped and the clouds were breaking up. Although the temperature had risen into the forties, there was still a damp chill on the late-afternoon air. It hadn't taken the paramedics long to arrive. Obviously well trained, they'd handled the rest of the delivery and cut the cord. They'd taken Kelly's and the baby's vitals. After giving each a cursory examination, mother and child were deemed stable and healthy and ready to transport. They were wrapped in warm blankets then lifted onto the gurney. Next, they were wheeled out to the ambulance waiting just outside the back door.

The little entourage didn't draw much attention. Traffic was practically nonexistent on the street out front, and other than Kelly's car parked in the middle of the parking lot, and Grey's sport-utility vehicle sitting in his reserved space near the building, the lot was deserted.

"I should go with you." It wasn't the first time Grey had made the suggestion.

She smiled tiredly. "You've already done more than I will ever be able to repay."

Repay?

"Excuse us, Judge."

Grey stepped aside, again.

What did Kelly mean, repay? She'd done all the work, suffered all the pain, and with barely more than a whimper, too. He'd helped deliver her baby, but had been useless ever since the paramedics had arrived. He'd been all that was between Kelly and total aloneness. Now he was in the way.

That didn't keep him from sticking close to the emergency vehicle while the paramedics got her and the baby secured, warm and comfortable inside. Any second now, they would close the doors. And then what? And then, nothing. His responsibility was over. End of story.

The first door clicked shut.

Grey slid his hands into his pockets for lack of a better place to put them. His feet were rooted to the pavement.

"Wait!" Kelly exclaimed.

This was more like it. Giving the paramedic a brief

nod and an uncustomary smile, Grey eased closer to the open door. "Yes?"

Weak and beautiful in the gray light of the dreary afternoon, Kelly nuzzled her daughter's tiny head, then said, "Thank you. From the bottom of my heart."

Grey felt a strange, swooping pull at his insides. He couldn't seem to speak, so he simply nodded.

"We'll take it from here, Judge."

He stepped aside for the last time. The paramedic closed the other door. The ambulance pulled away, leaving Grey standing alone in the parking lot in a puddle of melting ice, shivering, bare-chested inside his overcoat.

The wind blew through his hair, seeping through his clothing, reminding him that he couldn't stand here forever. Coming to his senses, he strode past Kelly's locked car, to his shiny, all-wheel-drive vehicle. His job was done. This episode was over.

It was time for him to go.

He wasn't sure where he was going even after he'd gotten in and started the engine. Perhaps it was the adrenaline rush, but he couldn't bring himself to simply go home. He considered paying his cousin, Sheriff Bram Colton, a visit at the sheriff station. The two men were friends as well as cousins, Bram on one end of law enforcement, Grey on the other.

The golden-brown brick station came into view. For some reason, Grey drove right on by. He was always welcome at his parents' house. Lately, Tom and Alice Colton had been feuding. A visit with them inevitably ended up with Grey's father saying, "Grey, tell your mother that..."

And Grey's mother saying, "Grey, your father can

speak to me himself, and until he does, you can tell him what he can do with his suggestion…''

No. Grey was in no mood to deal with his parents today. What then?

He drove past a pool hall called the Coyote. Instantly, an image of gray hair and wise eyes peering out of a lined, beloved face came to mind. Doing a U-turn, he headed southeast toward his great-grandfather's ranch near Waurika Lake.

Visiting George WhiteBear involved pursuit. It always had. And it was precisely what Grey needed to take his mind off Kelly Madison and the scrap of a baby girl born right into his own two hands.

He walked beside his great-grandfather on land that had belonged in the WhiteBear family since the early 1900s when the United States government developed a conscience and gave each Comanche family a portion of land to farm. In this day and age, a hundred and sixty acres was barely enough to scratch out a living on. George WhiteBear had never needed much. He raised some chickens, a couple of beef cattle and a few old horses that he rarely rode anymore. His three mongrel dogs were loyal, protective and showing their age. They had as much trouble keeping up with George as Grey did.

The black leather shoes he'd worn all day in court weren't exactly made for trekking through underbrush and wet weeds. Consequently, his feet were soaked, a two-hundred-dollar pair of shoes probably ruined. The outing had been worth a lot more than a pair of shoes. He and his great-grandfather were on their way back from a scrubby knoll where George had last seen the coyote he believed was his guardian spirit.

Grey had some of George's Comanche blood, and while he was intrigued by the ancient Native American ways and beliefs, he'd never experienced a visit from a guardian spirit himself. That didn't mean he didn't believe George had. There had been too many instances of late in which his great-grandfather had spouted wise words after encountering a dark-gray coyote with silver tips on his coat. Each time, the prophecy had come to pass. Secretly, Grey was relieved none of it had been focused on him.

The house, more ramshackle than run-down, was in plain sight when George stopped suddenly. He peered straight ahead, shading his eyes with a gnarled hand. Knowing better than to speak, Grey stood, quiet and motionless, waiting.

Finally, George lowered his hand. Pointing, he said, "The coyote waits. There."

Grey saw some brush move, but nothing more.

George stared straight ahead, as if straining to hear something of grave importance. Finally, he spoke. "The gray wolf hides from the truth."

George looked at Grey for so long that the hair on the back of Grey's neck prickled slightly. He scanned the weeds and underbrush surrounding his grandfather's house. Other than smoke curling from the chimney, nothing moved. He certainly didn't see a wolf hiding. And he didn't know what George was talking about. He couldn't have been talking about *him*, because Grey Colton had made it his life's work to flesh out the truth.

George said, "A wrong turn will lead the wolf to the right path."

Now Grey knew his great-grandfather wasn't referring to him. Grey didn't make wrong turns.

"Come," George said. "I cooked a fresh kettle of soup."

The two men completed the remainder of the walk to the house in silence. Once inside the old kitchen, Grey removed his wet shoes and socks and his overcoat. Rather than ask why Grey wasn't wearing a shirt, the old man went into his bedroom and brought out one of his own. Grey shrugged into it, then helped himself to a bowl of steaming vegetable soup.

To Grey, George WhiteBear had always been at once ancient and young. With his white braids and dark, lined face, he looked very much like his Comanche ancestors. He'd buried three wives, but the sadness at his most recent loss, his daughter, Grey's grandmother, Gloria WhiteBear Colton, was still fresh in his currant-black eyes. Neither spoke of it. They both understood that acknowledging it wouldn't lessen the pain or dull the loss. Only time would do that.

Beyond the windows, the sky darkened. Grey ate two bowls of piping-hot soup. Satisfied that George was well, Grey made noises about going.

"Unless the lone wolf has a hot date, stay."

Hot date? Grey laughed for the first time in hours.

George turned on his antiquated black-and-white television and tuned in the news. Grey's laughter evaporated the instant he glimpsed the woman on television smiling disarmingly from her hospital bed. Kelly Madison looked radiant as she told the reporter about becoming stranded in the courthouse, in the throes of labor, and how her daughter was born three weeks ahead of schedule.

The bloodhound reporter said, "I understand Judge Grey Colton helped you deliver the baby."

Grey sat up a little straighter.

Kelly smiled serenely and nodded. The reporter's smile was much less serene as she said, "Would you care to tell us what you and the judge were doing alone in the building?"

Grey held perfectly still.

Kelly executed a perfect yawn. After apologizing, she smiled again and confessed that she'd locked her keys in her car. "I do that from time to time. I don't know what Judge Colton was doing there. Working, probably. Thank goodness he was. It all happened very quickly. I was lucky to deliver so fast. At least the pain didn't last long. Have you ever had a baby?"

"Er, no, that is…"

"In that case, forget what I said about pain," Kelly exclaimed. "It's worth the pain, and more! You'll see. And now, I'm truly blessed to have a healthy baby girl."

"About Judge Colton," the reporter said smoothly.

Kelly blinked. "What about him?"

"How was he throughout the birth?"

"I don't really remember. I was a little busy."

"Did he hold the baby?"

Kelly nodded tiredly again. "Yes, but not for long. By the time the judge wrapped her in an old shirt, my cell phone was working. The paramedics came, and brought my precious baby and me to the hospital. The doctor said she has a big cry for a baby so small. Did I tell you she weighs six pounds and one-half ounce?"

"Yes, you did. Have you seen Judge Colton since he delivered your daughter?"

"No," Kelly replied. "Have you?"

"Er, um, no," she said. "Judge Colton couldn't be reached for comment."

In any other situation, Grey would have smiled.

"Do you think things will be strained between you and the judge the next time you and a client stand before him?"

Kelly pondered that, a faraway light in her soft green eyes. "I honestly doubt it. Judge Colton is a very fair and focused man. He's probably already forgotten all about what happened. My mother will never forget it or forgive me for having the baby without her. She and my father are driving out from Chicago sometime late tomorrow."

The baby started to cry from Kelly's arms, a lusty, hearty sound that brought the interview to an end. The reporter left Kelly to her child, ending the segment with a few facts regarding Judge Grey Colton's career, as well as speculation that he would hold a seat on the Oklahoma State Supreme Court someday.

The instant they went to a commercial, George switched off the television. A heavy silence ensued as he made an obvious perusal of the frayed and faded shirt he'd loaned Grey. He stared at Grey, an indecipherable look in his nearly black eyes.

Grey said, "If you would have asked what happened to my shirt, I would have told you."

George stood, shoulders stooped with age, hips thrust forward, legs bowed, hands slightly unsteady. "A wrong turn will lead the wolf to the right path."

The skin on the back of Grey's neck prickled again. What wrong turn? he thought, donning his overcoat and soggy shoes. He had an inborn sense of direction that prevented him from taking wrong turns. Hadn't he found his way out of mazes and blizzards? He'd navigated through law school and local politics and small-minded people in large groups. Grey had learned to work within each of those systems. His sense of direction had served him well.

He was a man, not a wolf. And he was calm on the drive back to Black Arrow. Although he hadn't been able to put Kelly and the baby out of his mind, he'd put them, and the situation, in perspective. In no time at all, mother and child would move to the back of his mind, forgotten except in those rare instances when some sight or sound triggered the distant memory.

Back at his house, he took a hot shower. Shirtless again, he padded barefoot to the kitchen. Portia, his housekeeper, had left the pot roast she'd prepared for his dinner in the refrigerator. Evidently, delivering a baby had stimulated his appetite. He made himself a thick sandwich, carrying it and a cold soda to his desk, where he planned to study some new changes in the law.

He wound up staring into space, marveling at the way Kelly had fielded the reporter's questions. He wondered how she and the baby were. Realizing it was futile to attempt to study the intricate changes in the state and federal laws tonight, he left his plate of crumbs next to his unfinished can of soda, and went upstairs. In his big bedroom, he donned a lightweight merino wool sweater, socks and shoes, and headed for his SUV.

The hospital corridor was quiet when the elevator door slid open. Following the arrows, Grey made his way to the maternity wing. Nurses glanced at him as he passed, but no one asked if he needed help. He knew the way, which further diminished his grandfather's statement that a wrong turn would lead to the right path.

Grey Colton simply could not afford to make wrong turns.

The door was open in the room at the end of the hall. All was quiet inside. Kelly was asleep. He paused, uncertain how to proceed. A dim light was on over her bed, casting shadows where her eyelashes rested above her cheeks. Grey couldn't help staring. His reaction was swift, powerful and instinctive. She was beautiful, and it wasn't just the color of her hair and lips.

He moored the balloons at the foot of her bed and left the bouquet of pink roses on the window ledge. Tucking the stuffed rabbit in the crook of his arm, he started for the bed, only to stop. He didn't know what he was doing here, and couldn't shake the feeling that he was walking on eggshells. Perhaps he shouldn't have come. She'd had a hard day, and he didn't want to disturb her.

He wished she would wake up.

A sound at the door drew him around. A nurse entered the private room nearly as quietly as Grey had. Glancing at her patient, she whispered, "It looks like the new mother is sound asleep. Are you a friend? Or relative? Or are you the father?"

It occurred to Grey that he knew nothing about the baby's father. He considered the other categories. "I suppose you could say I'm a friend."

Kelly's eyelashes fluttered, and her eyes opened. Grey started to smile.

"Judge Colton!" she said.

The smile never made it to his mouth. He would

never forget the pride he'd felt the first time someone had addressed him that way. Judge Colton. Tonight, he was disappointed.

"So you're the man who helped bring the baby into the world!" The nurse thrust a thermometer into Kelly's mouth, and held a stethoscope to her chest. Next her blood pressure was taken. After making notations on a chart, the nurse said, "Later, we'll get you up so you can take another walk. I believe Joanne is on her way with your baby."

As if on cue, another nurse entered the room, pushing a plastic Isolette in front of her. "I hear you've had a nice nap!" she exclaimed. "The baby's been sleeping, too, but I think she wants to see her mama now."

All eyes were on the child as the nurse scooped the infant up and deposited her into Kelly's waiting arms. The baby had been bathed, and was wearing the smallest white shirt Grey had ever seen. Her eyes moved beneath her closed lids, and her little lips parted.

"Alisha," Kelly said softly, "do you remember Judge Colton?"

The other nurse said, "Ring if you need anything, dear." Both left the room.

Grey finally completed the trek closer. "Grey," he said quietly, his gaze on Kelly. "After this afternoon, 'Judge' seems a little formal, don't you think?"

Kelly shrugged, nodded, shrugged again. She thought it was a good thing the nurse had finished taking her pulse, because it skittered alarmingly as she stared at the dark-haired, dark-eyed man who had delivered her daughter. Despite the comforting weight of her child in her arms, she was aware of a current in the air and a tingling in the pit of her stomach.

"Is something wrong?" he asked.

She shook her head. He handed the stuffed toy to Kelly, but didn't readily release it. For a long moment, they both held it. She looked up at him, recalling everything he'd done for her. He'd seen her at her worst. No man in his right mind could be attracted to her after that. That meant this was one-sided. She would have liked to deny even that. She'd just had a baby. Women who'd just had babies couldn't possibly feel attraction.

"Are you in pain?" he asked.

Physically, not really. Emotionally, he had no idea! But she shook her head a second time. What she was feeling was simply gratitude. And respect. Okay, maybe even genuine fondness.

Oh, dear. Genuine fondness wasn't good. Feeling genuine fondness for the judge had all the markings of a major complication.

Smoothing the wrinkles from the baby's blanket, Kelly reminded herself that she couldn't afford any more complications. She had her daughter to think about. This beautiful, precious child was all that mattered. It had been this way since the moment Kelly had discovered she was pregnant. The very fact that Alisha had been conceived hours before Kelly's divorce had been final was proof that when it came to matters of the heart, she didn't always make the smartest choices. Sealing the divorce with a kiss hadn't seemed like such a strange request when Frankie had made it. Despite all his faults, her ex-husband was a great kisser. Unfortunately, far too many women knew it. She'd loved him once, and he'd hurt her terribly. She had Alisha now, and she could no longer afford to allow her emotions free rein over her common sense.

Still, she didn't know quite what to make of the feelings swelling her heart this very minute. Serious and brooding, Judge Colton was the wrong kind of man for her. Not wrong in the same way that Frankie had been maybe, but wrong just the same. Frankie DeMarco was charming, fun-loving and the life of every party. He was everyone's friend. She'd learned the hard way that he was nobody's hero, especially not hers.

She stared at Alisha's tiny face, memorizing every feature. Alisha was hers, all hers. The nurses all said she looked just like Kelly. Maternal love washed over her with such force tears welled in her eyes.

"Do you want me to call the nurse?"

It had been an emotional day. Blinking back tears, Kelly studied the judge. He had a rugged physique, broad shoulders, a muscular chest. His facial features were dark and chiseled, striking and strong, his chin, his cheeks, his forehead. She didn't know much about his personal life, but today, he'd been her hero, which probably meant that this was hero-worship, and nothing more.

Smoothing the fine wispy hairs on the baby's soft head, she sighed in relief. "I don't need the nurse, thanks."

"Do you want me to leave?"

She shook her head. "You can stay awhile if you'd like."

Grey couldn't quite understand why he felt compelled to stay, but he did. He sat in the chair next to the bed and studied the baby. He'd never had much of an interest in babies. He couldn't seem to take his eyes off this one. "You named her Alisha?"

"I'd been tossing other names around these past months. William, after my grandfather, if she'd been a boy, Grace for a girl. After we got here, and the doctor checked us both out, I held her, and watched her sleep. And I kept thinking about the stories you told me when I was having her. About your mother, Alice, and your grandmother. I considered naming her Gloria, but Alisha Grace feels right."

"Alisha Grace," he repeated. "It suits her."

Kelly nodded. "Alisha, after your mother. Any woman who raises six children, one of whom didn't panic and was able to deliver a baby in his chambers in less than ideal conditions, deserves a special honor."

Somewhere down the corridor, a baby cried. Kelly's baby opened her eyes, as if curious about the sound. She was going to be smart, Grey thought. She was already observant. He touched her tiny hand. Instantly, she grasped his finger, her grip unbelievably strong for someone so small.

"Did you see the news?" Kelly asked.

He nodded, mesmerized by the baby's clear gray eyes looking up at him.

"I didn't think about the press," Kelly whispered, "or how they might want to do a story about what happened."

He hadn't, either.

"It was wise of you to be unavailable for comment."

Grey lifted his gaze, and found Kelly looking at him. Her makeup was gone, her face clean scrubbed. Her hair had been brushed, the overhead light casting shadows below her cheekbones and beneath her chin. Her eyes were clear and observant and very green above the faded blue hospital gown. Her nose was narrow, her mouth was…

Kissable.

He forced his gaze away and stood, the action tugging his finger from the baby's grasp so quickly he startled her. For a moment, he thought she was going to cry. He held his breath, releasing it only after the baby relaxed again, secure and safe in Kelly's arms.

"I wasn't really prepared to be interviewed," Kelly confessed.

"You handled it like a pro."

She smiled down at her daughter. Apparently in the mood to chat, she said, "I'm an attorney. You're a judge. Some people might read more into what you did for me and Alisha."

Grey scratched at the prickly skin on the back of his neck.

"They could even think I might try to use the incident to gain special treatment in court," Kelly said. "I assure you that that won't happen."

"Of course not."

"If you ever need a kidney, come see me." She wavered him a smile. "Otherwise, rest assured, it'll be business as usual."

She lifted her gaze, and held out her hand. Grey had a feeling that somewhere in the deep recesses of her mind, she knew exactly what she was doing. What did she mean it would be business as usual from now on? He took her hand, shaking it as if in slow motion.

Kelly's heart expanded, and something very close to sexual attraction uncurled in the pit of her stomach. She'd been experiencing mild afterbirth pains. This was different. It wasn't hero-worship, either. Oh, dear, she thought. This was bad. It definitely had all the markings of a major complication.

Only if she let it. She withdrew her hand from his grasp. "Thank you."

He bristled. "We both did what had to be done."

My, my. "I was referring to the flowers, the balloons and the plush toy for Alisha."

Silence. He wasn't happy, but at least she'd put whatever was between them back on an even keel. Now she had to keep it that way. "I guess I'll see you in court, Judge," she said.

"Grey." His eyes glittered, as if daring her to dispute it.

"But I thought we agreed..."

"You said it best yourself this afternoon. We've shared too much for such formalities, at least outside the courtroom."

"That isn't what I said."

"What did you say, then?"

She gulped, because what she'd said was that only a woman's doctor and her lover should see her the way Grey had seen her. Oh, no, he didn't. She wasn't going to repeat that.

He had the nerve to smile.

It was a nice smile, a masculine smile, a disarming smile that sneaked up on her, causing her to smile, too.

"Kelly?"

"Hmm?"

"You and I both know I'm not your doctor."

He walked to the door on silent footsteps, and Kelly was left with her mouth hanging open, her heart beating a heady rhythm, her mind reeling.

From the doorway, he said, "Call me if you need anything."

"That's what I was trying to… I don't think… That is, it would be best if…" She clamped her mouth shut, raised her chin. In a steadier voice, she said, "I won't need anything. I'll see you in court."

She caught his expression before he turned on his heel and left. Her point had hit its mark.

"I probably shouldn't have done that," she whispered, nuzzling Alisha's unbelievably soft cheek. "What else could I do?"

The baby started to cry. The *waaa-waaa* grew in volume until Kelly hugged her to her breast. Instantly, the crying stopped. That was easy, she thought, stroking the baby's head. When it came to her child, she just had to do what came naturally. The same did not apply to Grey Colton. And that was final.

Chapter Three

The courtroom was quiet as Grey studied the document in front of him. He made a notation, then looked straight at the man standing before him. "Forty hours of community service!" His decree was punctuated by one sharp rap with his gavel.

"But, Your Honor, this was my first offense…"

"Make it your last and we'll get along better in the future."

"But I thought—"

Grey silenced the young man with a quelling glare and a quiet question. "Would you like me to make it sixty hours?"

A buzz went through the people waiting to stand before Judge Colton for whatever misdemeanor they'd committed. The youngest judge in Comanche County was reportedly also the toughest. Although he was neither condescending nor self-serving, no one knew exactly what to expect. In the courtroom, he was swift, cutting, but just. Nobody cared to meet him in a dark alley. Especially not today.

The attorney answered for the young man who'd been caught red-handed desecrating public property. "No, Your Honor. My client will do his forty hours."

Grey caught the covert glance the attorney and his client shared. They'd been hoping he would be more lenient because the younger man's record had been clean up to this point. Earlier that morning, Grey had seen two attorneys on opposing sides share a similar look, obviously in unprecedented and total agreement: Judge Colton was even tougher than usual today.

They were wrong. It *was* possible that Grey was more abrupt, his tone sharper today, but his sentencing was fair, as always. He hadn't let his mood influence the punishment. If he had, the last woman, a shoplifter, would have gotten life.

The next case went quickly, as did the one after that. At ten minutes before twelve, Grey pounded his gavel a final time and broke for lunch.

"All rise!"

Grey gathered up his papers, strode past the bailiff, then retreated to his chambers. The second the door was closed, he removed his black robe. He ran a hand through his hair.

He was agitated. He didn't get agitated. Judges needed to be cool, calm and collected. They needed to be focused. They had to be able to sit for long periods of time without moving, their minds sharp, their knowledge of the law indisputable.

Grey approached every case as an important one. And every person who left his courtroom, be it drunks, petty thieves or those accused of far more serious crimes, got a crash course about the price he extracted from anyone who chose to break the law.

Judge Grey Colton had no regard or patience for dishonesty, and he'd never met an honest criminal. Lawbreakers made the world a dismal place. Except in very rare instances, there was no excuse for what they did. If it were possible to send all criminals to an island and let them prey on each other, America would need fewer judges. It didn't work that way. Criminals tended to be repeat offenders, and they preyed on innocent people. It was the innocent people Grey had vowed to protect. It was why he'd become a judge. Ultimately, it was the reason he had his sights set on a position on the Oklahoma State Supreme Court.

He'd charted his path in his early twenties. He was still on course a dozen years later.

He strode to the supple leather couch. For some reason, he wound up studying his hands. They didn't look any different; the palms were broad, his fingers squared at the tips. He'd held a child in them as she'd taken her first breath.

Until that moment, he'd thought that pounding a gavel was the most important function his hands could perform. He'd said it best to Kelly himself. He was no doctor. And he didn't want to become one. He didn't.

He liked what he did. He believed in what he did. He was good at what he did. He was agitated. That was all. And it had something to do with that baby. And perhaps her mother.

Kelly Madison had made herself clear. If he ever needed a kidney, she'd said, come see her. In other words, she would never forget what he'd done, but in everyday life, she was a defense attorney and he was a judge. She was a sunny sky. He was a gray storm. He was oil. She was a refreshing sip of water on a warm day. Oil and water didn't mix.

He went to his desk and sat down. He opened a folder and scanned a document. His gaze trailed to the wallet lying in the corner near his green desk lamp. The cleaning service had been here overnight. Evidently, they'd discovered the wallet under a cushion.

He picked up Kelly Madison's wallet, only to return it to the desk. He already knew what was inside. Her address for one thing, and a credit card and driver's license.

He was reaching for the phone to call a messenger service to deliver it to her, when the phone rang beneath his hand. "Judge Colton," he said.

"They're kicking me out."

He recognized that smooth, lilting voice. "Who is?" he asked.

"The hospital," Kelly said. "They're sending me home."

"You don't want to go home?"

"I want to. I'm scared to death, but my parents are due to arrive later this evening. It isn't that. It's just that none of my friends are at their desks, and my keys are still locked in my car. I would call a cab, but I seem to have lost my wallet. And I know what I said about you and me and business, but I didn't know who else to call." She took an audible breath. "They're kicking me out. Something about insurance."

"I'll be right there."

He shrugged into his overcoat, and dropped the

wallet into his pocket. He glanced at his watch as he left his chambers. "Nancy," he said to the poor woman in charge of the phone system during lunch. "I have to go out for a little while. I might be late for the first case. Stall them until I get back."

"Where are you going?"

The door closed behind him. Judge Colton was already gone.

Twelve minutes later, Grey strode into Kelly's hospital room. Kelly looked at him from the chair. "Judge, Grey, I..."

"If you thank me, I'll have a bench warrant put out for your arrest."

"On what charges?"

"Annoying a judge."

There was a short stretch of silence as she tilted her head slightly. "You and I both know you would never misuse your authority in that manner."

She believed in his integrity. He noticed she didn't thank him, though. The balloons he'd brought last night were tied to the handle of a paper bag. A car seat bearing the hospital insignia was on the bed. Kelly was dressed, the baby wrapped in a white blanket. "It looks like you're ready to go."

"Everything has happened so fast. I pray I can do this."

Grey didn't know what to say to that, so he didn't say anything. She rose carefully, and gently lowered the baby into the car seat. "I bought a special outfit to bring her home in. But it's at home."

"I won't call the fashion police if you don't," he said.

Kelly paused, and looked at him. And smiled. Grey

couldn't tear his eyes away. She was wearing the green knit dress she'd been wearing yesterday. He saw no sign of makeup today. She looked young without it, and fresh and pretty. The green of her eyes shone from her pale face. Her lips were full and naturally pink. Something about her brought out every male impulse he had.

"I was going to call a cab," she said, giving the room a careful perusal, "but as I said on the phone, I seem to have lost my wallet."

"You wouldn't have gotten far on two dollars." He reached into his pocket and handed her the wallet. At her look of surprise, he said, "The cleaning crew found it under a cushion in my sofa."

"And you went through it?"

He shrugged. "Not a bad photo."

"You looked at my driver's license."

He noticed it wasn't a question. "Height, five feet six inches. Weight, one hundred twenty-five."

Her color heightened slightly. "That was my pre-pregnancy weight."

He hadn't expected to laugh. He couldn't help it. Her honesty was refreshing.

A nurse clattered in, pushing a wheelchair. She set the brake, helped Kelly into the chair, then handed her the car seat, which now contained one sleeping day-old baby. "Ready?" she said.

"Ready," Kelly said.

Grey gathered the balloons, the flowers and the paper bag, and followed after them. In a matter of minutes, Kelly's and Alisha's seat belts were buckled inside his SUV, and Kelly was giving him directions to her house.

* * *

The baby slept all the way home. Kelly took turns staring at her sleeping child and looking out the window. It had felt like winter yesterday. Today, the sun was shining. Spring was in the air, a few broken limbs and power company trucks parked on the sides of streets the only signs that there had been an ice storm yesterday. The entire world had changed in twenty-four hours.

Twenty-four hours ago, she thought, carrying her sleeping infant up the sidewalk leading to her rented house, she'd been a pregnant woman. Now she was a mother. A mother!

A single mother.

"Have you thought about how you're going to get into your house without your keys?" Grey asked.

Moving very slowly and deliberately, she leaned down, retrieving a spare key from underneath a rock. She supposed there was one good thing about her bothersome little tendency to lock her keys in her car. She made sure she had spares.

Judge Colton, or Grey, mercy, she didn't even know what to call him, helped her inside. He'd made it clear that he didn't want her gratitude. Alone with him in her small living room, her sleeping child all that was between them, she didn't know what to say. It occurred to her that he didn't know what to say, either. She thought about that. Grey Colton at a loss for anything was a new concept.

He was wearing a black shirt and tie today, and the usual black slacks and shoes and overcoat. My, but he looked good in black. Yesterday he'd worn a white shirt. Now that she thought about it, she'd never seen him in any other colors. He was a black-and-white kind of man. Cut-and-dried. No shaded areas, no uncertainties. Kelly couldn't imagine that. When it came to her personal life, she never knew if she was making the right decision. Work was somewhat easier. At work, she trusted her instincts. Somehow, she just knew when a client was telling her the truth. It was too bad she didn't have the same success with relationships.

She sighed. "Well," she said, "you probably have to get back to court."

He made no move to leave. "It'll wait. It isn't as if they can start without me."

"At least it hasn't gone to your head."

She caught him looking at her, surprise in his eyes. There was something new, something different about Grey Colton today. Until yesterday, he'd never looked at her with anything other than tolerance and professional courtesy. She wouldn't exactly classify this new expression as open friendliness, but there was warmth in his eyes, and a lazily seductive gleam that reminded her that he'd carried her in his arms yesterday and helped her through the most difficult and perfect thing she'd ever done.

That feeling found its way to the pit of her stomach again. It was like a warm, swirling attraction, and it had no business being there. She needed to sit down.

"Do you have everything?" he asked. "Food? Diapers?"

She lowered gingerly into an overstuffed rocker and gently set it in motion. "My parents will be arriving later tonight. We'll be fine until then. You should do that more often."

Kelly hadn't meant to say that. She could practically hear the gears turning in Grey's head as he tried to decide *what* he should do more often. "I was re-

ferring to smiling, Grey. See? Once you crack those
facial muscles, it hardly hurts at all.''

The baby started to whimper. Grey stayed another
five minutes. After making sure Kelly had everything
she needed, he left, locking the door behind him.
She'd called him Grey.

He was halfway back to the courthouse when he
noticed she was right. He was smiling, and it hardly
hurt at all.

Grey wasn't smiling when he turned onto Kelly's
street at seven o'clock that evening. This wasn't exactly on his way home, so he couldn't say he was in
the neighborhood. Most likely, he wouldn't have to
say anything. He wouldn't even see Kelly tonight. He
would simply drive past and make sure her parents
had arrived.

He slowed as he neared her house. Finding her
driveway empty, he parked at the curb out front and
was on the porch before he could change his mind.
His knock on the door went unanswered. She probably couldn't hear it, what with all the noise the baby
was making. He tried the door. Finding it locked, he
rummaged underneath the rock for the key, and let
himself in.

''Kelly?''

She still didn't answer, but he knew where she was.
He could chart her progress through the house by the
ebbing and flowing decibel of Alisha's cry. They entered the room, Kelly's face pale, Alisha's red. The
new mother looked exhausted, and slightly relieved
to see him.

He was glad he'd stopped by.

Her hair was mussed, as if she'd only recently gotten up from a nap. She'd changed out of her green dress, and into what appeared to be leopard-print lounging pajamas. Evidently, she hadn't put on much weight these past eight months. Already, it was difficult to tell she'd ever been pregnant.

"How long has this been going on?" he called over the ruckus.

Kelly glanced at her watch. "About a half hour."

"What's wrong with her?"

Kelly brought her baby to her shoulder. Jiggling her, she crooned unintelligible words of comfort in her little ear. Alisha was having nothing to do with unintelligible words of comfort. "She's hungry," she finally said.

"Why don't you feed her?"

"I can't."

"What do you mean, you can't?"

Kelly shook her head.

Alisha cried louder.

So Grey shouted louder. "Why can't you?"

Kelly looked at Grey. She looked at Alisha. A tear squeezed from the corner of her eye. "Because my mmm...my mmmmm..."

"Your mmm?" Grey repeated.

"My m-m-milk hasn't come in yet." She burst into tears.

Grey was halfway across the room when the door opened and a middle-aged man and woman in neon colors rushed in. "Mom, Dad," Kelly exclaimed. "Am I glad to see you!"

The red-haired woman in stiletto heels rushed toward Kelly, kissing the air close to her cheek. "Oh, sweetheart, how are you?" She brushed her lips across the top of Alisha's head before hurrying down the hall. "I'll just be a minute, dear. Haven't used a rest room since Missouri. You know your father."

The gray-haired man tugged on his ear—was that an earring?—then glanced casually at Grey. "Made great time. Got pretty good gas mileage, too, all things considered." He kissed Kelly's cheek. "How are you, sweetie?"

Kelly's mother returned, instantly taking the squalling baby. The crying stopped. Grey figured Alisha was probably stunned by all that bright orange. And that was just her hair!

Kelly's father looked Grey up and down with mild interest. "Who are you?"

Grey considered several responses. He happened to glance at Kelly, and found her looking back at him. Something passed between their gazes, and he heard himself say, "I'm a friend of Kelly's."

"Not just a friend," she countered.

This time Grey was the one surprised.

"What I mean, Mom, Dad, is this is Judge Grey Colton."

"Judge?" her mother exclaimed.

Kelly nodded.

"*The* judge?"

She nodded again.

"So?" her father asked.

"So," his wife exclaimed. "This is the judge who delivered your granddaughter!"

Kelly's father slapped Grey on the back. "Good job!" To Kelly, he said, "Have you asked anyone to be godfather, yet?"

"No," Kelly said. "Why?"

He turned to Grey next. "Christenings are an important event in our family. And I'd say you've earned the privilege.''

"Daddy!" Kelly said.

"Vinnie!" Kelly's mother said.

"Vi!" Kelly's father said.

"Vinnie and Vi?" Grey asked.

"Vincent," the older man stuck out his hand. "My friends call me Vinnie. And the little woman over there is Vi, short for Violet.''

In her stiletto heels, the "little" woman was at least five-ten. And in that garish outfit, Violet was no shrinking violet, that was for darn sure.

"Grey Colton," Grey said.

"Nice to meet you."

Normally, it took a lot to make Grey's head swim. Vi and Vinnie had accomplished it with seemingly little effort.

"Hello, there, Alisha. What a pretty name." Vi's voice was singsongy. The baby was mesmerized. "So you were delivered in a judge's chambers, were you? You're a Madison all right. Did your mama tell you about your cousin, Lance, who was born in a taxicab during rush-hour traffic in L.A.? No? Well, he was. He's six now, but I still send that taxi driver a card every Christmas.''

Grey held perfectly still, imagining what it would be like if the only connection he had with Kelly and Alisha was a card at Christmas. He glanced at the baby, an unwelcome tension settling between his shoulder blades. What was wrong with him? This child was nothing to him.

There was a lot of gushing and gooing and ga-ga-ing after that. In almost no time at all, Alisha was drinking water from a bottle, Kelly was sipping warm soup, Vi was traipsing back and forth on her stiletto heels, and Vinnie was bringing in the luggage, lots and lots of luggage. From the looks of things, they were going to be staying awhile.

There was nothing for Grey to do. He might as well have been invisible. He told himself this was for the best. He would be seeing Kelly in his courtroom when she returned to work. He would ask after the baby from time to time. Meanwhile, he had enough to deal with. His parents were feuding, and except the twins, who were off to college, his siblings all seemed to be head over heels in love all of a sudden. Luckily, Grey was the focused one, the disciplined one. He would just leave Kelly to her parents and get on with his own goals.

Kelly, the baby and Vi disappeared down the hall, whispering something about breast feeding. That left Grey alone with Vinnie, who turned on the television and immediately immersed himself in pro-wrestling.

Still standing, Grey looked at the television where a man wearing a Tarzan suit pretended to body slam a three-hundred-pound man name Rosie. Rather than pull up a chair, Grey eyed the empty hallway. Slowly, he made his way to the door.

"Get up, you wimp!" Vinnie sputtered to the television, jumping to his feet.

Grey reached for his coat hanging over the back of a chair, and let himself out. The Madisons were a strange family. Strange or not, they were Kelly's family, and she was in good hands.

Kelly had no idea who was pounding on her door, but the fact that she could hear the knock all the way from the kitchen had her hurrying. Eight-day-old Alisha was asleep in the cradle in the living room. Kelly really, really, really needed her daughter to sleep for a little while longer.

The knock came again, rattling the glass in the door. She had no idea who it could be. She wasn't expecting company. Her friends were all at work, her parents at the store. It was too early for the mailman.

Her steps slowed at the first glimpse of the dark-haired man in the black shirt and tie standing on her doorstep. She'd told herself she'd imagined her reaction to Grey the day he'd brought her and Alisha home. Her heart fluttered wildly. She wasn't imagining her reaction to him today. She hadn't seen him in a week. Not that she was counting the days.

She took a deep, calming breath, ran her fingers through her hair and reached for the doorknob. The directions she'd been studying crinkled as she opened the door.

"Grey."

He looked back at her, his eyes dark and deep and steady.

"What are you doing here?"

"I just had lunch with Bram."

The breeze smelled of spring and felt refreshing on her face. "Bram Colton? Sheriff Bram Colton?"

Grey came in without waiting for an invitation. Projecting an energy and power she'd noticed before, he stopped just inside the door.

Her heart thudded once, twice, three times. "Does Sheriff Colton live near here?" she asked.

Was that her voice, so deep, so sultry?

"No."

"Then why..."

His eyes delved hers, his hair slightly windblown,

his tie a little crooked. He seemed in no hurry to reply. She thought she detected a flicker in his intense eyes. For a long moment, neither of them moved.

"I took a wrong turn," he said.

She had no idea why he suddenly clamped his mouth shut, as if he'd just confessed something of grave importance. Stepping around him to close the door, she glanced at her hand. She closed the door quietly, then turned, quickly hiding the apparatus and directions behind her back.

"What do you have there?"

"Nothing." She leaned back slightly.

He leaned closer. "What is it?"

"I told you it's nothing."

She took one backward step before backing into the door. He moved closer, so close that everything except his eyes blurred, and those dark eyes riveted her to the spot.

His right hand found its way around her waist. Her breathing hitched, a delightful shiver of wanting running through her. They stood toe to toe, her breasts nearly touching his chest. Something delicious uncurled deep in her belly. As if in silent answer, he lowered his face toward hers.

With a blunt-tipped finger, he lifted her chin. And she knew. He was going to kiss her.

She had about five seconds to decide whether or not she was going to let him. The clock was ticking.

Grey eased closer.

Chapter Four

Kelly would not kiss Grey Colton.

All she had to do was tell him. She would not kiss him.

She opened her mouth. She looked into his eyes. Her heart skipped a beat. He had the dreamiest eyes she'd ever seen. They were a deep dark brown, full of secrets just waiting to be explored.

Who was it who'd said it was the quiet ones you had to watch?

He tipped her face up slightly. Her heart tipped, too, and swelled, balancing precariously on her breastbone.

She shouldn't kiss Grey Colton. There were a dozen reasons why.

He made a sound deep in his throat, so masculine and intimate. Now, where was she? Oh, yes. There were reasons she shouldn't kiss him....

Weren't there?

She took a deep breath of air scented of soap and

springtime and man. Oh, my. She wanted to kiss Grey Colton.

Oh, dear.

Everything inside her went perfectly still. This wasn't simply a case of wanting to do something. She needed to kiss Grey Colton. Oh, dear, oh, dear, oh, dear.

She swayed slightly, and her eyes closed. As if it was all the invitation he needed, he touched his mouth to hers.

His kiss was slow and thoughtful, like him. He moved his mouth across hers, parting her lips, deepening the kiss, sending a surge of excitement through her. The only points of contact were their lips, his fingers beneath her chin and his hand at the small of her back. Delicious sensations started in each of those places, sending something warm and pleasing to her breasts, fuller these days, and to the pit of her stomach, where the sensation lingered, fluttering like butterfly's wings.

Alisha was sleeping in the bassinet near the sofa. Kelly was instinctively aware of the humming sounds her baby made in her sleep, as only a new mother could be aware of her infant. At the same time, she was aware of Grey, as only a woman could be aware of a virile, attractive man.

He was warm, bracing, sensuous. And yet he held his passion in check, just barely, keeping the kiss gentle. The hint of what he was holding back sent her heart catapulting into her stomach and her senses spinning. If she reacted this much to his gentleness, she could only imagine how she would react when he took it further.

If he took it further.

She couldn't let him take it further. She wouldn't let him. And she wouldn't let herself, either. Drawing back slightly, she finally managed to end the kiss. She opened her eyes, and found him looking at her, his eyes dilated, so that only a ring of brown encircled them. His nose was straight, his face all angles and planes and perfection. He took her breath away.

Her emotions were delicate these days. According to the books she'd been reading these past eight months, it was natural to cry easily in the weeks and months following childbirth. She didn't feel like crying. She felt like floating and grinning, and maybe singing. And kissing him again.

She held perfectly still, for feeling like this was dangerous. Hadn't she promised herself she wouldn't let herself get swept away ever again?

Somewhat disoriented, she was aware that he was reaching behind her. For one breathless moment she thought he might kiss her again. Again, she feared she would let him.

"About this secret contraption you're hiding." Slowly, he drew her hand from behind her back.

She stared dumbly at the apparatus held tightly in her hand, and at the long, masculine fingers wrapped securely around her wrist.

That was what the kiss had been about? He'd done it to throw her off balance so he could discover the answer to his earlier question? She'd been double-crossed.

Or had she?

His breathing was every bit as deep as hers, the expression on his face intense. An incredible magnetism had built between them, and she wasn't the only one who felt it.

"What is that?" he asked.

She stared at the item in question. "I'll tell you what it isn't. It isn't user friendly." She turned to look at him, and felt trapped by the intensity of his gaze. Rolling her eyes and shaking her head, she said, "If you must know, it's a breast pump."

"A what?" He looked incredulous.

She knew the feeling. "You heard me."

"You mean…"

She nodded. "I have an appointment with a client tomorrow. My parents are going to watch Alisha. And my daughter doesn't like to be kept waiting when she's hungry."

"Have you…"

"Not yet. I was going to, before you arrived." She'd been trying to figure out how to use the pump. She hadn't had much luck, which was why she'd gone back to the directions. And then Grey had shown up. Any minute now Alisha was going to stir. And Kelly still hadn't mastered the procedure.

"It seems painful."

"So? I'll do anything, no matter how painful it is, if it's best for Alisha." She glanced at Grey, and caught him looking below her shoulders where her bustline was straining the buttons of her blue knit shirt. His eyes closed partway and a muscle worked in his jaw. He tore his gaze away, but it returned, lingering like a caress.

That fluttering sensation was back in the pit of her stomach. Her breasts tingled, but not the way they had earlier when he'd kissed her. She recognized this tingling. Any second now…

She turned on her heel. "If you'll excuse me."

"Where are you going?"

Casting her sleeping daughter a look on the way by, Kelly rushed down the hall without answering Grey's question. She wasn't going to need those directions after all.

In her bedroom, she closed the door, opened her blouse and unfastened the special closure on her nursing bra. She used the pump, letting nature take its course. It was a slow process, but a necessary one. The important thing was to stay relaxed. She let her mind wander. Of course, it went straight to that kiss.

She'd been completely carried away by her response to Grey's kiss, and on the same day she'd sworn she would never be vulnerable to any man ever again, too. She was attracted to Grey. It had come out of the blue with enough force to buckle her knees and melt her resolve. Watching the creamy liquid that would sustain her child in her absence, Kelly told herself she could deal with attraction. She would ignore it, or pretend it didn't exist, until it didn't.

Alisha deserved the best Kelly could give her. She deserved sustenance. For all intents and purposes, she didn't have a father. Kelly was all her precious child had. That made it even more important for Kelly to make the right, the best choices from now on.

And from now on, she would resist Grey Colton's allure. She would tamp down the attraction. She would...

She was halfway finished with the pump when she heard the first peep out of her daughter. As usual, it didn't take Alisha long to work up to a full-scale wail.

Oh, dear. Kelly wasn't done.

Too bad there was no off switch on the breast pump. She peered around her bedroom, as if for guidance. Instead of guidance, she heard silence. The crying stopped.

Kelly went to the door and listened intently. She could hear the quiet murmur of Grey's voice. It grew stronger, then weaker, and it occurred to her that he was walking around the living room. She opened her door a crack. She still couldn't make out the words he was saying, but he seemed to be talking to someone. Her heart expanded again, because he was talking to Alisha. And her child had stopped crying to listen.

"That's right," Grey said, walking slowly, the baby held stiffly in both hands. "You don't want to cry. And you don't want to interrupt what your mom's doing. Trust me on this one. Tomorrow, you'll be real glad you did."

He'd nearly panicked when the baby had started to cry. Deciding he couldn't very well leave while Alisha was screaming, and obviously Kelly couldn't stop in the middle of what she was doing, he'd reached into the bassinet. After fumbling a little with the blankets, he'd picked her up awkwardly. She'd let him know she expected him to do better next time. But she'd stopped crying. Now he moved carefully around the room, the baby held out in front of him, her head supported in one hand, her back in the other.

He swore he'd had sandwiches that weighed more than she did. Before last week, he'd never held a baby so small in his life. His younger brothers, Shane and Seth, were twenty. Vaguely, he remembered carting them around, but he'd been thirteen or fourteen, and they were Coltons, which, among other things meant that they'd entered the world half-grown. At least that was what Grey's mother always claimed.

This was a strange time to be thinking about his mother. But suddenly, he had a whole new appreciation for Alice Colton. What he felt for her little namesake here was different.

Alisha's eyes were gray. Her skin had lost its redness. Her cheeks were creamy white, and for the first time, he noticed that she had soft, wispy brown hair. Her ears were unbelievably tiny and perfectly shaped, her nose a button, her lips full, like Kelly's.

"That's right," he said, being careful not to jiggle her or drop her as he moved around the room. "We'll just have us a little talk and a nice walk while your mother takes care of business."

The baby was wearing tiny white pajamas with pink bears on the collar, cuffs and feet. She looked comfortable and precious and small. Adorable.

Alisha stared back at him, unblinking, and it was as if she was thinking, *Go ahead and admire me. In fact, take all the time you want.*

She brought her little hand to her face, and wound up smacking herself with it. She let out one squawk in protest, but didn't cry.

"You're going to be strong, aren't you? The kind of person who could roll with the punches. In the meantime, you need to work on those muscles and your coordination," he said. "It's only been a week. Don't worry. You'll get it figured out."

She turned her head, as if to look at him from a slightly different angle. He learned that she made a different noise with every movement, as if it required concentration and effort. She always found him with her gaze, though. And once she did, she stared at him.

He wondered if she remembered him.

He told her about some of the cases he'd tried recently. Halfway through a particularly intricate case, she yawned. "Am I boring you?"

She stretched, making more racket, and Grey chuckled, surprising himself. She didn't seem surprised at all. Again, she homed in on him with her steady gaze.

"You keep your gaze that steady and you'll make a good judge someday."

She blinked. Her mouth skewed to one side, then evened out. Her lips lifted a little, and then a little more. Why, it almost looked like a smile.

Something was happening to his chest. He was either having a heart attack, or he was being charmed and beguiled by a female who didn't even weigh seven pounds.

A door rattled in the back of the house. Within seconds, Vi and Vinnie bustled inside through a back door. "Hello, Judge!" Vinnie said.

"Where's Kelly?" Vi said at the same time.

Before Grey could answer, Kelly's mother traipsed over and reached for her granddaughter. "Who has Nana's precious princess?"

"She just smiled at me." Grey had no idea why he'd said that.

"Babies this young can't smile." Vi eased the baby into her arms.

She made it look so easy. How did women do that? "She smiled," Grey said more succinctly this time.

"It was probably gas," Vinnie insisted.

Unbeknownst to anyone, Kelly watched from behind the ficus tree in the hallway. Although Grey had relinquished Alisha to Kelly's mom, he couldn't seem to take his eyes off her daughter.

A tear squeezed out of Kelly's eye and ran down her cheek. Another one followed.

Great. Now she cried.

Trying not to sniffle, she crept back to her bedroom. She could hear her father talking about the Red Sox. She heard Grey leave soon after. Kelly missed him already. No she didn't.

She liked him. Okay, she admitted that much. She liked him.

She liked Grey Colton. She appreciated Grey Colton. She would even go so far as to admit that she was extremely attracted to Grey Colton. All the more reason to nip this in the bud. Which was exactly what she would do the next time she was alone with him.

Kelly and her client took a seat at the polished table. Other than the two of them, the only people in the courtroom were her client's mother, the police officer who'd made the arrest, the prosecuting attorney and the bailiff who stood near the door.

Today's session was only a formality during which the judge would determine whether there was enough evidence to proceed. Kelly's client was an eighteen-year-old boy—okay, a man in the eyes of the law—who'd been arrested and charged with breaking and entering. The incident had occurred at his seventeen-year-old girlfriend's house. It was no coincidence that it had been the girl's father who was pressing charges.

It was a classic Romeo and Juliet story.

Like the majority of her clients, Brian Jones's family barely had the money for rent, let alone thousands of dollars for an attorney. Brian looked skinny and nervous and young in the suit coat his mother had gotten for him at Goodwill. The prosecuting attorney and his client both wore suits that cost more than Brian's mother made in a week. The opposition was smug in their silk ties and Armani shirts.

Brian looked as though he was going to throw up. She felt for the kid, but let him fidget. It would aid in the element of surprise she had up her sleeve.

"All rise!" the bailiff called.

Without sparing a glance at her client or the competition, Kelly rose to her feet. Judge Grey Colton entered the courtroom and took a seat behind the bench. He moved with an animal grace that was somehow at odds with the black robe.

The preliminaries were dealt with quickly, the case number stated, the charges spelled out. Judge Colton asked the attorneys if there was anything he should know before continuing. The prosecuting attorney said rather smugly, "I believe everything is spelled out in black and white, Your Honor."

Grey nodded. Finally, he looked at her. "Ms. Madison?"

She rose to her feet. "There is one thing, Your Honor."

The prosecution looked on as if bored.

"My client was never read his rights, Your Honor."

The other attorney jumped to his feet. Judge Colton leveled him a look every attorney in Comanche County recognized. Outbursts were not tolerated in Judge Colton's courtroom.

"Do you have proof of this?" Grey asked.

"Yes, Your Honor, I do."

"What proof?" the attorney client exclaimed.

Grey pounded his gavel once in warning.

"It's right here, Your Honor," Kelly said in a quiet yet firm voice. "May I approach the bench?"

Grey motioned both attorneys forward. Kelly glided around the table, taking a signed statement with her. Handing it to Grey, she said, "The police officer who failed to read my client his Miranda rights is here. If necessary, I have two other witnesses who were present and are willing to testify to the fact as stated in that signed document."

Grey commended himself for his steady hands as he took the legal document from Kelly. Next, he motioned the police officer in question forward. While the man was in the process of complying, Grey's gaze strayed to Kelly.

Her auburn hair was up, her makeup understated. Her black blouse looked soft, her gray skirt and jacket professional-looking. The top two buttons of the jacket weren't fastened. For a split second, his gaze lingered there. Something restless and unwelcome stirred inside him.

"Your Honor?"

His lips thinned with anger. No one needed to know it was directed at himself. He sent the attorneys back to their respective corners, read over the document, then asked the young police officer if he had anything to add.

"No, Your Honor." The officer didn't look much older than the defendant.

"Case dismissed!" Grey pounded his gavel, stood and left the courtroom.

He was aware of opposing sentiments from the few people present today. He didn't make eye contact with any of them.

"Give me ten minutes," he said to the bailiff on his way by, his robe fluttering.

"Yes, Your Honor."

Grey closed the door just short of a slam. What the hell had happened to him in there? He'd gotten sidetracked. It hadn't been sexual. Exactly. It had been more like a distant cousin to sex, caused by a new, nodding acquaintance he had with foreign objects such as breast pumps and babies' booties. The truth was, he hadn't been the same since he'd delivered that baby. And he didn't know what to do about it.

A knock sounded on the door on the opposite wall. "Yes?" he called.

The door opened, and Kelly entered. "We need to talk."

For a second, he thought she'd noticed him looking at her breasts earlier. That was unlikely, for she seemed more nervous than angry.

"What did you want to talk about?" he said.

"About…yesterday."

"What about it?"

Kelly was rarely at a loss for words, and yet she found herself discarding the words spinning through her mind, one after another. Was Grey being purposefully obtuse? This was the first time she'd been in his chambers since she'd had her baby here. It would have been understandable if that was the reason she was having a hard time continuing. Except that wasn't it.

Grey hadn't removed his black robe. Standing there in his office, he looked tall, powerful, as forceful as the balance of justice he represented. He was a formidable presence in street clothes. The robe only added to the persona.

The fact remained that he had another case to hear. And she had Alisha to hurry home to. Therefore, this had to be said. And soon. "We need to talk about that kiss."

He held her gaze, but made no attempt to further the conversation. He *was* being purposefully obtuse.

"Kissing is..." She wet her lips. The movement snagged his attention. Suddenly, her lips felt pouty and sensitive. "It isn't..."

"Yes?" he said.

"A good idea." Her gaze went to his. There was no reproach in his eyes, but there was warmth, and a lazily seductive gleam that reminded her of the way he'd looked yesterday just before he'd kissed her. And just after.

"Which?" he asked.

"Pardon me?"

"Kissing is a good idea, or it isn't a good idea?"

"It isn't."

"I disagree."

Had he taken a step closer?

"But...?"

Or had she?

"Why do you disagree?" she asked.

"Because," he said, "I want to kiss you again."

She gasped. "You can't."

"I know."

The room was so quiet the shuddering breath she took echoed in her own ears. "We're both at work."

"I know that, too."

Okay, now he sounded condescending. *That* rankled. She crossed her arms, and caught him following the movement with his gaze. He had no business looking where he was looking. To his credit, he didn't stare for long.

"I didn't say I would, Kelly. I just said I wanted to."

His voice sounded huskier.

"We have to work together." Heaven help her, her voice sounded huskier, too.

"Are you saying we should forget that kiss yesterday?"

She heaved a huge sigh. "Yes."

"Can you?" he asked.

Her relief was short-lived. She swallowed.

"Because I don't think I can," he said. "In fact, I'm sure."

"How on earth can you be sure?"

"Because," he said quietly, his black eyes glittering, daring her to dispute it, "I've tried."

Oh. He'd tried. Oh, dear. The buzz of an electric drill carried from the construction crew that was putting the finishing touches on the renovations to the county courthouse. The sound only added to the vibration deep inside her.

"But it's wrong," she said.

"What is?" he asked.

She swallowed again. "You are."

For the second time in a matter of minutes, Grey's ability to think coherently deserted him momentarily. He didn't remember the last time anyone had told him he was wrong. He didn't much care for it now. "I am?" He finally asked. "I'm wrong?"

She nodded.

"What are you talking about?" he asked.

Her eyes suggested innocence one second, and ancient wisdom the next. Something told him he wasn't going to like what she was about to say.

"I've given this a lot of thought. You're a wonderful man. What you did for me. And for Alisha. There's no way to thank you enough." She held up a hand in a halting gesture. "And I already know you don't want my thanks. Which brings me to the facts. And the fact is, you're wrong for me."

She waited for him to speak. Taking his silence as her cue, she turned on her heel and quietly left.

Grey didn't have the luxury of that particular option. He had a docket full of cases to hear. He paced the small room, going over the conversation in his mind. Kelly had been thinking about that kiss. And she'd come to the conclusion that he wasn't the man for her. He couldn't agree more.

He filled a glass with water, drank half of it, then emptied the glass and turned it upside down next to the sink. He dried his hands. Whatever fleeting connection there had been between him and Kelly was over. Perhaps now he would be able to concentrate.

Kelly heard a vehicle pull into her driveway at shortly after six. At first, she thought her parents were returning from the grocery store. Luckily, she'd finished feeding Alisha. Kelly was glad she was becoming more adept at getting herself all tucked back in, because it wasn't her parents at all. It was Grey. She could tell by the sound of his knock. It was abrupt, controlled, and still threatened the integral structure of the old wood door.

He entered without waiting to be invited.

Continuing to rock Alisha, Kelly lifted her daughter to her shoulder and gently patted her tiny back, waiting for the burp. She breathed in the sweet smell of innocence. She loved rocking her baby, loved the sound of her daughter's breathing, the feel of that moist air on Kelly's neck. She relished the weight of that little body, the heat of her skin. Grey looked warm, too, only his heat appeared to be coming from under his collar.

He was angry and agitated. He did an admirable job holding it in check. Pinning her in place with his stare, he closed the door behind him and said, "What do you mean I'm wrong for you?"

Kelly opened her mouth, clamped it shut, then tried again. When it was clear that all she could do was stammer, he started toward her, closer, and closer, until she had to tip her head back from her position in the chair in order to look at his face. She stopped rocking. Continuing to gently pat Alisha's back, Kelly waited for Grey to continue.

"I repeat," he said, his voice deep, his enunciation perfect. "What do you mean I'm wrong for you?"

Alisha chose that moment to burp. It was a big sound for someone so small. It broke the silence, and the tension, at least for the moment. It also bought Kelly a little time.

Rising carefully to her feet, she eased around Grey

and padded to the bassinet in the corner. Alisha barely stirred as Kelly laid her down and tucked a lightweight blanket around her.

Straightening, Kelly turned from her daughter.

And came face-to-face with the judge.

Chapter Five

"What are you doing here, Grey?" Kelly spoke in a hushed tone so as not to startle Alisha. It had been raining when Kelly had gotten home from the court-house earlier that afternoon. About an hour ago, the rain had turned into a fine mist. Now, at a little after six, it looked as if the sky was clearing.

Staring at Grey, it wasn't difficult to see where the clouds had gone. Obviously, he hadn't come straight here. Tiny drops of moisture sat on the shoulders of his suit coat, and further darkened his hair. Storm clouds churned in his eyes, but his voice remained quiet and steady as he said, "I've already told you why I'm here. I'm curious about something you said in my chambers today."

He stood statue-still, his feet planted, his arms crossed. Something told Kelly he could stay that way for hours if necessary.

"What do you want me to say, Judge?"

"Grey."

She sighed. "Grey."

"What's wrong with me?"

His lips thinned, and it occurred to her that he probably hadn't meant to word the question in exactly that way. Normally, he was in control, not prone to sudden outbursts. If he were anyone else, she'd make light of it, asking if he wanted the list alphabetically or in order of importance. But he wasn't anyone else. He was Judge Grey Colton. He ruled his courtroom with a just but heavy hand. He rarely smiled, let alone laughed. Those were traits not faults. And really, she didn't know him well enough to know his faults, which brought her to honestly say, "As far as I can tell, there's nothing wrong with you."

"That's not what you said in my chambers."

"That's true." She skimmed her hand up the arm of her silk blouse, bringing her fingers to rest at her throat.

"You said I'm wrong for you."

Her throat convulsed beneath her fingertips. "That's true, too."

His eyes darkened dangerously.

Biting her lip, she glanced around her small living room. She didn't want to anger this man. She didn't really want to ask him to stay, either. She simply couldn't imagine making small talk with Grey Colton. In the end, her manners won out, and she said, "Would you care to sit down?"

Grey kept his expression even and his gaze steady. He took a chair near the window, when what he felt like doing was chewing glass. Kelly lowered herself to the couch. She'd taken her hair down after work. Grey remembered removing the pins when she'd been in labor. He knew the texture, the way the waves felt beneath his fingers. He wanted to touch her again. He wasn't well.

She'd kicked off her shoes and removed the gray jacket. She was still wearing the charcoal-gray skirt and black blouse, although the blouse was untucked now. She looked comfortable, upbeat, pretty. He wished she would stop being so agreeable. He wanted an argument, a shouting-at-the-top-of-his-lungs, knock-down drag-out fight. And that was completely out of character. Grey Colton didn't argue. He didn't even raise his voice. Oh, but this woman pressed his buttons.

He wished she would press her soft body to his.

It was worse than he'd thought. Not only was he not well. He was a fool. She'd just had a baby. She'd just told him he was wrong for her.

Her kiss had said something else entirely. And that was why he was here.

It would help if he could forget about that kiss. It would help if he wasn't so aware of her every move, of the rise and fall of her chest with every breath she took, and the slight strain the movements put on those little buttons on her blouse. It would help if he had some other place to look.

A movement out of the corner of his eye caught his attention. He turned his head in time to see a teenage boy disappear around the side of the house. Instantly alert, Grey sprang to his feet and headed for the door.

"Where are you going?"

"Stay in the house." He reached the door. "And lock this behind me."

Grey moved quickly, quietly through the wet grass the way his great-grandfather had taught him when he was very small. Rounding the corner, he came up behind the trespasser before the kid knew he wasn't alone in the backyard. Grabbing a rather bony shoulder, Grey hauled the kid around.

The boy came up swinging. Grey's arms were longer, stronger. The boy was strong, too, and obviously surprised to have his plans thwarted.

"What the hell are you doing, Judge? Le'me go!"

He knew Grey was a judge? There was something familiar about the portion of face not covered by a baseball cap. Where had he seen this boy before? Probably in court.

"What do you think you're doing?" Grey asked.

"What do you think you're doing?" Kelly said at the same time.

Grey had spoken to the teenager, but Kelly was talking to Grey! She hadn't stayed in the house. She'd slid into her shoes and hurried after him. Stopping a few feet away, she glared at him.

"For heaven's sakes, let him go."

Grey didn't appreciate that tone of voice. It made *him* feel like the criminal here. "I saw this kid slinking around your backyard. He's probably casing the joint."

"I wasn't." The kid's blue eyes were big and round now. He was trying to back out of Grey's grasp. "I swear I wasn't."

"I know. It's okay, Brian," Kelly said.

Grey was getting a bad feeling about this. Brian? Kelly knew him? In a flash, it dawned on him where he'd seen this young man. It had been in court, all right. That very day. This was the kid with the fresh haircut and secondhand suit who'd been accused of breaking and entering, the kid who'd gotten off because of improper procedures.

"I'm sorry, Brian," she said. "I didn't know what the judge was going to do until it was too late. I ran out here as fast as I could."

The boy said, "You just had a baby. You're not supposed to move fast." His eyes narrowed at Grey for a moment in an expression of accusation and extreme dislike. "What's he doing here, anyway?"

Kelly wished she knew how to answer that. First things first. Placing a hand on Grey's arm, she said, "Let him go, Grey. He isn't doing anything wrong."

He loosened his grip, but didn't release Brian completely.

"Brian wasn't casing my place," she said. "He's doing yard work."

"You hired him?"

She smiled at Brian, but not at Grey. "If you must know, yes, we're working out a trade."

Grey unhanded the young man. Brian straightened his T-shirt and rubbed his shoulder. He still didn't look any too happy. "Do you want me to do anything else today, Miss Madison?"

She looked at the fallen branches he'd stacked and the rocks he'd piled over in one corner of her yard, and finally at the lanky young man who needed a break in life far more than she needed to be paid in cash. "Can you come back tomorrow to do more?"

He nodded, and started away with a lope people in Kelly's generation just couldn't imitate.

"Brian?"

The boy paused at the sound of Grey's voice. It was clear he didn't want to give the judge the time of day. Kelly wondered what on earth Grey was going to do next. He walked toward Brian. Stopping a few feet away, he said, "I owe you an apology."

Brian wasn't the only one whose mouth dropped open.

"I was wrong to jump to conclusions, and I'm sorry." Grey held out his hand. After interminable seconds, Brian took it. They shook hands. And Kelly noticed that when Brian walked away this time, it wasn't with a lope.

Her anger dissolved like vapor in the onrushing wind. And that wasn't good. Her anger had served an important purpose, allowing her to rein in her feelings and hold Judge Colton at bay. She'd always been a firm believer in two surefire cures: a hearty laugh and a good night's sleep. She hadn't been getting much sleep since she'd brought Alisha home, and she couldn't have laughed right now if her life depended upon it.

There were layers to Grey Colton's personality. He wasn't all cut-and-dried, as she'd once thought. He represented justice, but wasn't above apologizing when he was wrong. She didn't know many *people* like that, let alone many men.

Grey was tall, solid as a brick wall, but underneath, now, that was a different story. He wasn't all rock and brick inside. He wasn't mush, either, but along with the rock and brick were layers of goodness and kindness and hesitancy and self-consciousness. It was those inner layers that intrigued her, drew her most.

The breeze blew a lock of hair into her face. Grey lifted a hand to brush the strand away. She was accustomed to people touching her hair. The color, wave and texture had always drawn people's attention. But no one had ever touched her the way Grey was touching her now. He didn't sift his fingers through the long tendrils. Instead, he took a thick portion in his hand. Holding her still, holding her spellbound, he curled his fingers around a thick swathe, squeezing it as if the softness and thickness were unlike anything he'd ever touched before. Except he had touched her hair before. That day, in his chambers, when Alisha had been born.

She should be getting inside. She'd put on shoes before rushing outside, but no jacket. Although spring was in the air, there was a damp chill in the breeze that sent goose bumps chasing up and down her arms. Underneath, she felt warm, and airy, and hopeful, as if the day was brimming with possibilities.

She lifted her face to the sky, inhaling the scent of rain-washed earth. What was wrong with her? Nothing about the past ten minutes should have made her feel this way, and yet she felt happy and dreamy and yes, very womanly. Surely it was hormones. What other explanation could there be for this attraction that she swore she didn't want or need? The closer she came to knowing Grey, the closer she came to wanting him, and wanting was a dangerous thing for Kelly, especially at this point in her life, especially when the man in question was the judge of Comanche County.

"He's working off his fee, is that it?"

She blinked, turned her head, and came back to earth. Who? What fee? What was Grey talking about? And then it dawned on her. He was still talking about Brian.

She bristled and took a backward step, then watched as his hand fell away from her hair. "Why is it that as soon as I start to like you," she asked, "you go and say something that makes me mad?"

"So you do like me."

She waved as if at a bothersome insect and returned to the matter at hand. "We were talking about Brian."

"Yes, we were. It would take the boy months, perhaps years' worth of yard work to equal the amount of money you could have made with a paying client."

"His mother's going to help, too." She clamped her mouth shut and asked herself why on earth she'd said that. She didn't owe him any explanations.

"In what way?"

She was suspicious of the expression on Grey's face. He had no right to question her or pass judgment, and yet she found herself saying, "Clara Jones is going to watch Alisha part of the time."

"Do you think that's wise?"

She straightened her back and narrowed her eyes. "If I didn't, I wouldn't have asked her, now, would I?"

"What do you know about this woman?"

She turned, stomped toward the back door. She made it as far as the gravel driveway before she stopped suddenly, and turned again. Only she came up short, because Grey had followed her and now stood less than two feet away. A woman really needed to put a bell on this man. The idea brought back a semblance of calm and rationale.

"Yes, it's wise. And I'll tell you why. Clara is proud. She has good reason to be. That woman doesn't let anything beat her down, at least not for long. She's thirty-five years old and has an eighteen-year-old son. She's raised Brian by herself, working her butt off to put food on the table and save up enough money so both of them can go to the local community college in the fall. He's a good kid, too. But he could have been ruined by his girlfriend's father. Can you imagine what might have happened if he'd actually gone to prison?'' She shuddered. ''Now Clara believes I can walk on water. She can't afford to pay me, and I need someone caring and compassionate and trustworthy, yes, trustworthy, to watch Alisha from time to time. Any more questions, Judge?''

She noticed he let the ''judge'' title go this time, but it had hit its mark. His lips thinned in annoyance.

''I assumed your parents would want to watch Alisha.''

''They're leaving tomorrow.'' When he remained mute, she said, ''This is what I meant earlier. If I were looking for a man—I'm not, but if I were—I would look for someone who doesn't believe the worst of people.''

''Meaning I do?'' His voice was deeper than she'd ever heard it.

She didn't want to hurt him. She didn't want to hurt anyone, but it had to be said. ''Yes, Grey. I'm sorry, but I'm afraid you do.''

''Now you're the one who's wrong.''

Leave it to Judge Colton to tell her she was wrong. ''I'm not.''

''You are.''

She planted her hands on her hips and shook her head. This was getting them nowhere, so she said, ''What am I wrong about?''

He inched closer. ''I don't believe the worst of everyone.''

She looked up at him. A car drove by out front. Farther away, kids' voices were raised in play. Much closer, Grey's voice had been low and sincere and as smooth as red velvet. The shallow lines in his face added to the overall symmetry of his square jaw and angular cheekbones. His chest expanded beneath his white shirt. A muscle worked in his jaw, but he didn't say another word.

Unable to help herself, she said, "Who do you believe in, Grey?"

"I believe in a lot of people."

"That's nice, Grey." She should have known he wouldn't give her a straight answer.

"And I believe in you."

Her arms made an X across her chest to help prevent herself from melting. "You believe in me?"

He nodded once. If he smiled, she would crumple. But he didn't smile. She melted a little anyway.

"We're opposites."

He conceded the point. "Opposites attract."

Kelly felt a headache coming on. She knew how opposites could attract. Her attraction to her ex-husband had been a crash course on the subject. She'd learned her lesson. Only problem was, Grey was nothing like Frankie. That didn't mean he was right for her.

"It takes more than attraction," she finally said.

"I agree."

He did? He had the nerve to smile at her surprise. Regaining her composure, she said, "It takes similar interests, backgrounds, beliefs."

"I'd like to explore those." He spoke without looking away, his eyes dark brown and warm and deep enough to slip into.

"I don't think that would be a good idea, Grey."

"Why?" As usual, he didn't waste words.

"We're opposites."

"We've already established that. I'm a man, you're a woman. We can't get much more opposite than that."

"Yes," she said, "but hear me out. You're serious."

"So?"

"Shh. You're serious. I'm spontaneous."

"I like spontaneity."

"Sure you do. And your eyes are blue." She clamped her mouth shut, wishing she hadn't mentioned his eyes, which were an intoxicating shade of brown. Now that she had, she couldn't seem to look away. Again.

His eyes were deep and contemplative, the edges crinkled slightly as if in pleasure. That was when it occurred to her that he was enjoying this.

"You don't believe me?" he asked.

She shook her head. "When was the last time you did anything spontaneous?"

He was looking at her lips.

"Something that doesn't have to do with this unholy attraction that seems to have sprung up out of nowhere between us."

Grey recognized the rush of blood in his ears. He knew the cause. He'd been thinking his latest act of spontaneity had to do with kissing. He liked the way she put it better. Unholy attraction sounded slightly naughty and perhaps just a little forbidden. That only made the idea more desirable.

This wasn't simple lust here. There was nothing that elemental about it. An unholy attraction was far different than lust, and much more than an innocent kiss. She was right about that, for there had been nothing simple about their kiss.

He'd driven here three times without being invited. That was spontaneous. It was also completely out of character. He didn't mention it, because ultimately, it was also tied up with attraction.

He couldn't think of a single other incident. In his defense, normally, he couldn't afford to be spontaneous. He was a judge, and someday he hoped to be appointed to the Oklahoma State Supreme Court. His aspirations didn't leave a lot of leeway for spontaneity.

It was as if she knew. She looked at him far longer than he considered polite, then she looked a little more. Finally, she said, "Whose idea was it to climb onto that barn roof when you were a child?"

His eyes narrowed as he thought back. "It was mine. Why?"

"Good. Maybe there's hope."

She smiled, slow and thoughtful, and Grey realized she was laughing at him. He realized it. He understood it. What he didn't understand was why he felt no anger.

She took a step to one side on her driveway. He was still reacting to the sunshine that had a way of emanating from her, when the first splash of rainwater splattered onto his pants.

She stomped her foot again, sending more water his way. Grey felt something give within his chest. Without waiting to analyze what it was, he stomped his foot, too. She shrieked, jumped back, and stomped again. Rainwater, muddy now, went everywhere.

She shrieked again, and he chuckled, then broke

out in laughter. She joined in, at the same time getting in the last splash.

Gently grasping her arm, he drew her away from the puddle. The gesture was for his own protection, but it was to steady her, too. She'd just had a baby, after all.

They stood shoulder to shoulder, looking down at their mud-and-water-spattered clothing. "That's the second pair of shoes I've ruined this week."

His words drew Kelly's gaze. The subtle look of amusement in his eyes found its way inside her chest. It seemed like a long time before she was able to look away.

"Maybe you're right," he said.

He must have heard her gasp of surprise.

He smiled again, slow and thoughtful and deep. "Maybe there's hope for me yet."

She nudged him with her shoulder. "I'm glad you see it my way."

"Women are always glad when men see things their way."

"Are you an expert on women, too?"

"Are you crazy?"

She noticed he'd ignored that little "too." Wise man, Grey Colton. This time she was the first one to smile. "I need to go check on Alisha." She started for the back steps.

She'd reached the top stoop when he said, "Kelly?"

She looked at him over her shoulder. "Yes?"

"What would you say just happened here?"

Her glance swept over him from head to toe. His shoes probably were ruined, his pants, too. He didn't seem to mind. In fact, he looked happy and more lighthearted than she'd ever seen him.

She pulled a face as she considered her answer. Finally, she said, "Before we splashed in that puddle, during, or after?"

"Yes."

With a roll of her eyes, she said, "I'm not sure, but I think we're becoming friends."

His eyes showed his initial surprise before warming to the idea.

"Well," she said, still breathless, "I really do have to go inside."

"Of course."

"I guess I'll be seeing you."

"Yes, I guess you will."

She disappeared inside her little house. Slipping off her wet and muddy shoes, she padded to Alisha's bassinet. Her daughter was sound asleep. Staring at that perfect little face and the adorable contours of her growing seven-and-a-half-pound body nestled snugly beneath a soft pink blanket, Kelly wondered what she'd just done.

Whatever it was, her heart was still beating a little wildly as a result of it, and she was certain her face was flushed. By splashing Grey, she'd challenged him to be spontaneous. And he'd taken the challenge.

She'd thrilled in that. Heavens, she was still breathless! There was no going back now. Of one thing she was certain: Serious or spontaneous, Grey Colton was going to be an intriguing friend.

Grey's eyes jerked open. He lay there in the dark for a full second, uncertain what had awakened him. The telephone jangled a second time. He rolled over in his big bed. He had an unlisted number, and a phone call in the middle of the night—he squinted at the clock—at three o'clock in the morning set off alarms in his head. Clumsily, he reached for the phone. The remote hit the floor and the lamp teetered.

"Grey Colton."

"I'm sorry to bother you."

He went up on one elbow. "Kelly?"

"Oh. Sorry. Yes, it's me. Kelly."

"What's wrong?"

He listened intently. There were no sirens in the background. And Alisha wasn't crying.

"Nothing's wrong, per se. I was wondering if you would do me a favor," she said.

"What is it?"

"I have to go out."

"At three o'clock in the morning?"

"Yes. My parents went back to Chicago. And I can't take Alisha with me."

"Where are you going?"

Her pause was audible. He figured she'd awakened him from a deep sleep. Therefore, the question was legitimate.

"Um. Well. That is, to jail."

"What?" He imagined her holding the phone away from her ear at his outburst.

"I'm not actually going to jail."

He started to relax.

"I mean, I'm going to the county jail, but not to stay or anything."

His relief was short-lived.

"I'm going to bail out a client. And the county jail is no place for a newborn during the day, let alone in the middle of the night. And my parents are gone, and it's Friday night, and my two closest girlfriends aren't home. I didn't know who else to call. And we are friends now. Would you mind terribly?''

They'd been what she called friends for less than a week, and actually, he would mind *terribly,* not because of the inconvenience, but because he didn't like the idea of her going off into the dark for some shady client. He was already reaching for his pants. ''I'll be there in ten minutes.''

He was there in nine and a half, and he spent every second of those nine and a half minutes rehearsing what he would say to convince her that the county jail was no place for *her* in the dead of night, either.

It was a dark night without stars or a moon. There were no streetlights in this section of town. Every house on her street was dark, except Kelly's. The bare bulb of her porch light nearly blinded him as he hurried up her porch steps.

''That was fast,'' she said, opening the door before he had a chance to knock.

Her hair was secured at her nape with a wide clasp. She wore a burnt-orange blouse, brown pants and a matching blazer, a big sunflower pin on the lapel. She looked bright-eyed and bushy-tailed, while he still felt like yawning and scratching his chest.

''Attorneys don't wear sunflower pins on their lapels.''

At least she stopped picking up things and looked at him. Now that he had her attention, he got down to the business of talking sense into her. ''This isn't a good idea, Kelly.''

She glanced at the pin.

''Not the pin. What you're doing. Where you're going.''

"I know what I'm doing, Grey."

Okay, so he admitted that the way she said his name made his mind foggy again, but only momentarily. "It's three-fifteen. Whoever is in jail can wait until eight. Who is your client this time, anyway? A drug dealer? Or a drunk driver?"

He could practically hear her vertebrae click into place as she straightened her spine. "Do you want to watch Alisha or don't you?"

"I said I would, didn't I?"

And that closed the subject, at least for the time being.

She ran through a list of simple instructions, showing him two baby bottles, one containing boiled water and the other milk, a stack of disposable diapers that were unbelievably tiny. She wrote down her cell phone number, and the home phone number of Alisha's pediatrician.

"How long are you planning to be gone?" he asked.

"An hour, tops." She relaxed, even smiled. "I was feeding her when the phone call came from the jail. She shouldn't be hungry for two hours, at least. I appreciate this, Grey, which is why I probably do owe you an explanation."

She spoke as she packed her notebook and checkbook into her leather bag, which apparently doubled as a diaper bag and briefcase. "Technically, this woman is Mr. Walker's client. Since Cecil and his wife Georgeanne are out of town for the night, the call was forwarded to me."

Grey knew Cecil Walker. Not personally, but professionally. The man was sixty, reed thin, and wore the same black-rimmed glasses he'd worn thirty years ago, which just went to show that eventually every-thing came back in style. Except he hadn't done it to be stylish. He wore them because he was notorious for taking cases and clients who couldn't pay, there-fore he probably couldn't afford a new pair of frames. His clothes were even older than the glasses.

Grey didn't know why the hell it rankled, but it did.

He listened as Kelly told him how to warm up a bottle, and how to check the temperature on his wrist. After demonstrating, she asked, "Do you have any questions?"

"There's no way I can talk you out of this?"

She cast him what he'd come to realize was *the* look.

"In that case," he said, wondering why he was whispering, "good luck. And for God's sake, be care-ful."

She glanced at her sleeping daughter. He looked at the baby, too.

"She'll probably sleep the entire time I'm gone. I hope she sleeps the entire time I'm gone."

"Don't worry," Grey said, feeling confident. "We'll be fine. If she wakes up, I'll take care of her. How hard could it be?"

He didn't know what to make of her skeptical ex-pression. "You're sure?"

"Yes."

"I'll hurry."

"You do that."

She whispered a kiss on Alisha's forehead, slipped into her coat, reached for her briefcase, then left via the back door. Grey heard her car start, saw the lights flicker off the living-room wall as she backed from her driveway.

He wandered around the living room after that, wondering what he was going to find to do with himself until she returned. A faucet dripped somewhere. He considered fixing it. Aside from jiggling a handle or tightening a washer, he wasn't very good at plumbing. Besides, he didn't have any tools with him, and had no idea where Kelly kept hers, if she even had any.

He reached for the remote, flipped through the channels. He was just getting interested in a late-night talk show about the time he heard the first peep out of Alisha. When he checked on her, she appeared to be sleeping soundly. Grey went back to the interview on television.

Alisha's second peep was more like a grumpy-sounding grunt. In no time at all, she started to fuss.

He turned down the volume via the remote and strolled on over to her bassinet again. Evidently, he hadn't been quick enough, because she skewed her little face up and started to cry. Make that scream.

He picked her up. It didn't help. Of course it didn't help. He was stiff, and when he jiggled her, it was more like a bumpy car ride. He decided to put her to his shoulder and walk around with her. The only thing that did was bring her cry closer to his ear.

He didn't panic. She was just a baby. He was a grown-up. Kelly said she'd just been fed. So she couldn't be hungry. Maybe she was wet. He cringed a little at the thought of what else might be making her uncomfortable, then laid her down on the sofa and fumbled around for the snaps in her pajamas.

She cried, her arms and legs flailing and jerking,

her face red. The diaper was still clean and dry. Unfortunately, he'd ruined it trying to get it off her. By the time he finally got another diaper to stay on her, she was madder than ever, and his forehead was sweaty.

"You didn't cry this much the first time I held you," he said, picking her up again.

Lo and behold, she quieted a little. It must have been his voice. He kept talking and walking. The more he walked and talked, the calmer she became.

"Atta girl," he said, wondering how much longer before Kelly would be back. He glanced at his watch, then brought it to his ear. The watch was working fine. Ten minutes? Kelly had only been gone ten minutes?

He told himself not to panic. While he was at it, he told Alisha not to panic. They would get through this. It was only another fifty minutes or so.

This baby business was even harder than it looked.

Kelly shivered against the predawn chill as she pointed her car toward home. Bailing Cecil's client out of jail had taken longer than she'd thought it would. Everything always took longer in the middle of the night.

Grey would probably have twenty questions ready for her the moment she walked through the door. She had to remember not to divulge any information. He was the judge, after all, and it was important that Cecil's client has a fair trial, when the time came.

Yawning, she hurried as fast as she could, keeping within the speed limit, of course. The first thing she noticed as she pulled into her driveway was the lights shining from the kitchen and living-room windows. She wondered if that was a bad sign.

Alisha was an angel during the day. She slept, she ate, she studied the ceiling and the wall and the light. During the wee hours of the past three nights, she'd developed an attitude. Kelly had mentioned it to her mother over the phone yesterday. Violet had assured her that it was nothing to worry about, saying that all babies went through stages at two-week intervals.

Kelly let herself in her back door. All was quiet. She breathed a little easier with every step she took. She tiptoed to the archway connecting the kitchen to the living room.

What appeared to be several disposable diapers, the tabs torn off, littered the floor near Alisha's bassinet. A bottle lay on its side, dripping water onto the carpet. Another bottle, this one containing milk, sat on the end table near the sofa where Grey and Alisha slept.

She paused, her head tilting automatically, her arms gliding around her own waist. Grey was sprawled on the sofa, his neck cocked at an uncomfortable-looking angle, his feet dangling off the other end. His shirt was untucked, his knees bent as if trying to fit. His hands were folded over Alisha's little back, who was sound asleep on his chest. Both looked warm, peaceful, safe.

Something shifted in Kelly's chest, slowly spreading outward like waves on sand. The lights were on, the television screen in a blue holding pattern. She strode closer. Aiming the remote, she pushed a button, and the television screen went blank. Next, she tiptoed to the couch.

Leaning down, she tried to ease Alisha from under

Grey's hands. The baby didn't budge. Gently, carefully, she began unlacing Grey's fingers.

She happened to glance at his face. His eyes were open, his gaze roaming across her features, moving to her lips, to her throat, and lower. She froze in that position, bent at the waist, inadvertently awarding him a view he obviously liked.

She might have straightened if she could have. She would never know, because somehow, her hand had ended up in his.

Chapter Six

Kelly was aware of her surroundings, of the telltale signs of what Alisha had put Grey through tonight, that precious baby, herself, asleep on his chest. Her awareness of Grey was different. It felt more like a hum in the atmosphere. It reminded her of the thrum of a bass drum in the distance, too far away to be heard, but strong enough to be felt. The furnace was running. Out in the kitchen, the refrigerator clanked on. This hum wasn't coming from either of those things. It came from inside Kelly, spreading warmth, heating her from scalp to toe.

Her hand felt small in his, and yet she didn't feel weak or powerless. She felt...beautiful. It made her voice sound a little breathless in her own ears as she whispered, "I should put Alisha back in her crib."

He eased up a little on the hold he had on the baby, but not on the hold he had on Kelly's hand. "What time is it?"

"Four-thirty."

Their gazes locked.

"It took longer than I expected." His eyes continued to delve hers. Kelly felt the strangest swooping pull on her insides. "My darling daughter put you through the paces, did she?"

He squeezed her hand, making circle-eight patterns on her wrist. "Does this go on every night?"

"It only started a few nights ago." Kelly was still bent over, her hand in Grey's, her heart beating a steady rhythm, her chest brimming with emotions she was hard-pressed to name. "What did you finally do to get her to go back to sleep?"

"I called my mother."

He sounded sheepish about that, and Kelly smiled. "Did she come over?"

He shook his head. "She talked me through it over the phone."

Kelly straightened a little, and drew what felt like the first deep breath she'd taken since entering the room. "That was nice of her."

He shrugged. "She answered the phone in the spare room, which meant she and my father aren't sleeping together these days."

She noticed his grimace, as if he didn't know why he'd shared that particular personal tidbit of information with her. "She didn't mind being awakened in the middle of the night?"

"Not as long as she gets to meet Alisha."

Kelly smiled. And since she never tired of showing off her baby, she said, "I think that could be arranged."

"I'll tell her. Is it my imagination," he said, sitting up, bringing Alisha with him, "or is Alisha's cry louder at night?"

Kelly smiled again. "According to the experts in the books I've read, she's experiencing separation anxiety."

"Is that serious?"

She shrugged. "They say it's normal for a baby to have crying jags, and nothing we do seems to help."

"No kidding."

Again, she shrugged. "They say she just misses riding around in her own little safe haven where she spent the first eight months after conception before being so rudely thrust into the bright and cold world."

"People really write books about this stuff?"

"You wouldn't believe what the experts have to say about everything."

"An opinionated bunch, are they?"

"Experts are nothing if not opinionated, yes. So far, I've found that much of their advice is over-rated."

His eyebrows shot up.

And she said, "Why would Alisha only get separation anxiety in the middle of the night?"

"You don't believe everything you read."

He'd made it sound like a compliment. She wished it didn't make her heart swell so.

Grey didn't know if the stiffness in Kelly's back had finally broken through the haze of attraction between them—for she'd straightened, finally—or if her common sense had finally won out. She placed a hand at the small of her back, then took Alisha from him. The baby didn't so much as flutter an eyelash as Kelly put her back in bed. Grey wondered if the baby experts would say all that crying had exhausted her. He knew what the experts would say about what was happening to him.

He swung his feet off the couch and stood, almost all in one motion. Using the time it took Kelly to cover the baby and fuss with an extra quilt, he jiggled the loose change in his pocket and paced to the far side of the room. Back in control of himself, he took a closer look at the way he'd left the living room. Taking care of a newborn was a lot tougher than it looked.

Kelly began tidying up the place, talking as she went. "Your parents are having marital problems?"

He knew he shouldn't have mentioned his parents' personal trials. "You could say that."

"How long have they been married?"

Grey did not want to talk about his parents, not when something restless and far more enjoyable had come to life inside him.

His silence failed to deter her. "Are you worried they'll get a divorce?"

"My mother says murder, maybe. Divorce, never." Grey found himself mumbling, "I know just who would defend her."

She laughed quietly from across the room. She had a throaty, sultry laugh that caused Grey to wonder how she would sound in the throes of passion. She glanced at him suddenly, and caught him looking.

He strode toward her purposefully. She held up a hand in a halting gesture. He took it, of course.

"Grey. I don't..."

"You don't what?"

Her creamy throat convulsed. "We agreed to be friends," she said.

He nodded.

"I was prepared to be your friend."

"Was?" he asked.

She wet her dry lips. "Am prepared to be your friend."

"Are you this attracted to any of your other friends, Kelly?"

"No." She didn't appear happy about it, though. In a quiet voice, she asked, "Are you?"

"No."

Grey knew he'd better get out of there before she talked herself out of this. First, he said, "What time shall I pick you up tomorrow?" He glanced at his watch. The action gave him an excuse to pretend he didn't notice the set expression carving itself into her face. "Technically, it's already tomorrow."

"Grey."

"So technically, I guess the question is this. What time shall I pick you and Alisha up later today to go see my mother? You did just say that could be arranged, did you not?"

"Yes, I suppose I did say that, but…"

He didn't blame her for looking dazed. He'd honed his communication skills a long time ago. They served him well in court. It was just as rewarding putting them to use in his personal life.

"Get some sleep. We can decide on a time later."

He left then, taking with him a better understanding of those dark smudges beneath her eyes. He also had a deep-seated conviction that whatever he was feeling went deeper than friendship.

"Grey! Do you not own a telephone?" Kelly stood in the doorway at two o'clock that afternoon, a hand on her hip, a determined expression on her face.

Grey stood on the top step, looking far from innocent. He'd shown up at her door uninvited and unannounced. "You're the one who told me I need to be more spontaneous." He entered without waiting for an invitation.

She stepped to one side then closed the door. "I'm not ready to take Alisha to your parents'. I would have told you that if you had called before coming over."

And give her a chance to come up with an excuse not to see him?

"I didn't stop by to take you and Alisha to my parents' house."

"You didn't?"

He shook his head. "My mother would love to meet you—and Alisha, but she can wait."

"Then why are you here?"

Now, *there* was a question. He looked at her closely. Her hair was mussed, her face pale, making the dark circles under her eyes more pronounced. He'd conceived this plan on the way home at four forty-five this morning. "I thought you could use a break."

"A what?"

"Exhaustion is affecting your hearing."

She stuck her tongue out at him. But at least the old spunk was back.

"I thought perhaps I could take my goddaughter off your hands for an hour."

"Your goddaugh…"

He cut her off. "You're exhausted. It's no wonder."

"You really want to take Alisha for an hour?"

He nodded, and Kelly felt herself softening. She couldn't tell if he'd been serious about that goddaughter crack. After all, she hadn't asked him to be Alisha's godfather. Her father had. Grey wouldn't expect, couldn't think...

All that aside, Kelly was curious enough about Grey's other suggestion, the one about giving her an hour-long break, to ask, "What on earth would you and Alisha do for an hour?"

"Go for a drive? It's a beautiful Saturday afternoon. Or I could take her back to my place where she could listen to my theories regarding the latest changes in the law. She is a good listener, when she isn't screaming her head off."

Kelly stifled a yawn. "That's true. What if somebody sees you? They're bound to ask whose baby she is. What will you say?"

"I'd tell them the truth."

"You would?"

"That she was left on my doorstep by aliens."

She smiled tiredly. "Ah, honesty."

He stared straight into her eyes. "All kidding aside, I wouldn't lie, Kelly. Honesty is in short supply these days."

Something in his tone of voice bothered the back of Kelly's mind. "But what would I do for an hour?"

"Run for Congress?"

She rolled her eyes.

And he said, "Take a nap?"

Oh, the very thought was intoxicating.

Evidently, he took her yawn as acquiescence. "Do you have any more bottles? I know I saw diapers around here in the middle of the night. What else do I need?"

She wound up answering his questions, and adding about a hundred instructions regarding Alisha's care. It really was kind of him to think of her. Kelly trusted him with Alisha. She wasn't certain how that had happened, but as she bundled up her daughter, then carried her outside, she knew it was true. He followed with the supplies. It took him a few minutes to get the car seat out of her car, and into his SUV. She showed him the proper way to buckle Alisha in. And then Kelly was standing back, waving, and Grey and Alisha were driving away.

Kelly didn't move until they were out of sight. Shivering, she finally went back inside, but she couldn't seem to forget the way Grey had looked at her as he'd said that honesty was in short supply these days. Honesty was important to him. It was important to her, too, of course. But...

That "but" remained in the back of her mind after she'd slipped out of her shoes and lain down on her bed. She would talk to him about it when he returned in an hour. Ah, she had an entire hour...

Pulling the throw around her shoulders, her mind drifted, and her body relaxed. Her bed was so soft. In an hour, she would talk to Grey about...

Something...

Grey considered not answering his doorbell the first time it rang. Alisha was sleeping in his arms, and he didn't want to disturb her.

The doorbell rang a second time. And a third.

Since whoever was ringing it apparently wasn't going to go away, he put Alisha down on the sofa and surrounded her securely with pillows, then hurried to his back door. He found his only sister, Sky, standing on the stoop, in the process of ringing the doorbell a fourth time.

"It took you long enough." Wearing a fringed

jacket and skirt, Sky sauntered in as if she owned the place. Her clothing was typically southwestern, and yet she made the outfit look trendy and upscale. Besides being the only girl in the family, Sky was by far the most creative of his siblings. A talented jewelry designer, she'd recently become engaged and was now dividing her time between Black Arrow and Houston. "Guess who I just ran into?"

Since strolling in as if she owned the place *and* failing to call first were common Colton practices, he decided not to mention them. "Who?" he asked.

"Renee."

"Renee Lewis?"

Sky shrugged out of her lightweight jacket and continued as if clarifying was unnecessary. "She was extremely curious about what you've been up to, so I take it she isn't the reason none of us have seen you lately."

Grey leaned against his kitchen counter, crossed his ankles and held up what remained of a pot of cold coffee. She wrinkled her nose in distaste, then lowered into a chair, agile and perfectly content to be doing most of the talking.

Eyeing the doorway leading to the quiet living room, Grey decided there wasn't much he could do except wait for her to wind down.

"What's wrong?" she asked, catching him.

"What makes you think something's wrong?"

She looked him up and down with her gray, artist's eyes that saw far too much and made him glad he'd put Alisha's bottles in the refrigerator. "Because you're whispering. Are you hiding a woman somewhere?"

He hadn't realized he'd been whispering. He

cleared his throat and said, "Do you really think I'm the kind of man who would hide a woman anywhere? What are you doing here? How's Dom?"

Smiling, she said, "Dom's wonderful." It was just Grey's luck she didn't launch into her favorite topic: her upcoming marriage to Dominic Rodriguez, a burn specialist from Texas. Instead, she continued in her earlier vein. "You really aren't interested in Renee Lewis?"

A long time ago, Grey had grown accustomed to his family's matchmaking. They were all guilty of it, even their great-grandfather, with his prophecies and penetrating stares. Of all the Oklahoma Coltons, Sky and Willow were the most like George WhiteBear, especially when it came to their unnerving, probing looks. A long time ago, Grey had learned to deal with them by staring back, unblinking.

Sky threw up her hands in exasperation. Grey smiled to himself. Actually, Sky wasn't his first visitor today. Their cousin Bram, had seen his lights on, and had stopped in shortly after Grey had arrived back from Kelly's house before dawn. Bram had been curious about what Grey had been doing, too, although instead of wondering if he was seeing Renee again, he'd looked Grey up and down and declared, "All right, what gives? And don't try to deny it, because you have the dazed, sleepy look of a man who's just climbed out of a woman's sheets."

To which Grey had replied, "I wish." It was true. That in itself was cause for concern, not because he'd been having some stimulating fantasies about a woman, but because the woman was Kelly Madison, a woman he knew very little about. And Grey Colton simply didn't fantasize about women he hardly knew.

But that wasn't something he could tell his cousin or his only sister. So he said, "How is Renee?"

Sky rolled her eyes. Strumming her fingers, most of which contained a ring of her own creation, she said, "Oh, she's the same. Quiet, smart, unremarkable, other than her big Texas hair, boring."

Sky clamped a hand over her mouth, and eyed her older brother. "Unless you're seeing her. Then scratch that from the record."

He let her squirm for a minute, then shrugged, letting her off the hook. "I'm not seeing Renee, Sky."

She breathed a sigh of relief then changed the subject, talking about how bad things were getting between their parents. Grey's mind wandered. In a sense, his sister was right about Renee Lewis. Quiet and subdued, she kept her pretty features arranged in perfect order. She had an MBA from the University of Texas, one older, slightly pompous brother who was a urologist in Boston. Grey had dated her a year ago. Everyone said she was perfect for him. Except Sky, and Bram. And his parents, although they, at least, had been discreet about it. And really, they all would have accepted her if he would have chosen her. Maybe he should have continued to pursue her. She agreed with him on everything, and would have been a wise choice for the wife of a man who planned to have a seat on the Oklahoma State Supreme Court one day. They liked the same foods, the same music, books and art. Standing there in his kitchen, while Sky rattled on about their parents, it occurred to Grey that he'd seen Renee with her hair down only once. Even then, he'd felt no stirring of interest to explore the texture or the thickness.

She'd never splashed in a puddle with him.

She didn't believe every hardened criminal had had a tough break, and she didn't bail people out of jail in the middle of the night. She didn't have a baby, but no husband, either. He wondered about that. Not about Renee, but about Kelly. She never mentioned her ex-husband. In his experience, women always talked about their ex-husbands, even if it was just to say something scathing in passing. Renee had never been married. Just one more reason why she was perfect for him. There was only one problem. She bored him to death.

"Have you been over there lately?" Sky asked, reminding Grey that she was still talking about their parents. "They don't even speak to each other. I know we all agreed that the ten million dollars that was discovered in that account in Washington D.C. after Grandmother Gloria died should be used for an honorable, charitable function. But I'm beginning to think we should use some of it to send Mom and Dad on a world cruise or something. Then they'd have to get along."

"Just between you and me," Grey said, "I'd just as soon keep them away from any large bodies of water right now."

Sky sighed. "You're right. Mom would probably try to toss Dad overboard."

Sky and Grey shared a smile at the thought, for it wasn't really *that* bad. Thank God.

"I'll talk to them," Grey said.

Sky was rising to her feet when the first little squawk came from the other room. She paused. Pushing her long black hair behind her ears, she said, "What was that?"

Thinking fast, Grey said, "What was what?"

"Did you get a puppy?" She pulled a face. "Of course you didn't. As if the Honorable Grey Colton would ever get a puppy."

That rankled.

"Is the television on?"

Before he could decide how to reply, Alisha squawked again.

Short of blocking her path, there was nothing Grey could do to keep Sky out of the living room. He followed much more slowly.

She'd stopped a dozen feet from his sofa. Stared. "*What* is *that?*"

"What does it look like?"

"It looks like a baby."

Sisters. Grey brushed past his.

"That's what she is. A baby." Since he knew from experience what could happen if Alisha's hunger pains went ignored, he picked her up and carried her into the kitchen. He was getting the baby bottle out of the refrigerator when Sky joined him. Her eyes took on a dreamy quality.

"Whose baby is she?"

"A friend's."

Sky sashayed closer. "The same friend who went into labor during that ice storm?"

"Then you heard."

"It was all over the news, Grey. May I?" She took the baby while he warmed the bottle.

"I didn't know you knew anything about babies. I mean, you've always been so structured. Straight A's in high school. Straight A's in college. Then law school. You followed that up with an impressive prosecution record, which led to your current position as the youngest man in history to become judge of Comanche County. Next stop, the state supreme court. And along the way, you'll meet a woman as pure as the driven snow. When did you have time to learn to care for a newborn baby?''

She made him sound superficial, stuffy, and worst of all, as boring and predictable as Renee Lewis. It hadn't been boring or predictable to splash around in a puddle last week, or to help bring this baby into the world.

''There's nothing wrong with setting goals, Sky.''

''Sometimes the best things happen when we're not looking,'' she said, her eyes on the baby in her arms.

That sounded a little like his great-grandfather's latest prophecy: The gray wolf hides from the truth.

Sky looked a little surprised that he wasn't arguing with her, not surprised enough, however, to give the topic a rest. ''This is me. The kid sister who once found the list you used to rate women.''

''That was years ago.'' He took Alisha, positioned her at the proper angle in his arm and offered her the bottle. She clamped onto the nipple.

''You're saying you could fall in love with a woman with a skeleton or two in her closet?'' Sky asked.

''Sure. I guess.'' Although he doubted it would happen.

''What about marrying her?''

Grey thought about that, about how many politicians' careers ended because of past mistakes, and what a field day the press had with those skeletons Sky talked about. He didn't answer. And he really didn't appreciate the smug expression on Sky's face.

''Know what I think?'' she asked.

''I don't have a clue.''

"I think you ought to revise your list. The next time you meet a woman who can make you laugh, make you angry, make you crazy, you should marry her, skeletons and all."

She stared at him, waiting. He was thinking about a woman who made him laugh, made him angry, made him a little crazy. Mostly, he was wondering if Kelly had any skeletons in her closet. But telling Sky that would only give her more reason to lecture.

"What? No comeback?" she asked.

"I've discovered that generally speaking, people aren't learning much when their mouth is moving."

She clamped her mouth shut. He'd hit a nerve. He knew she was sensitive about the fact that she was the only one of their siblings who didn't have a degree, per se. She handed over the pink blanket she'd been fingering. Without saying a word, she headed for the door.

"Sky?"

She was halfway there when she turned stiffly.

"I'll take what you said under advisement. And you and I both know you're smarter than any of us, and don't need a degree to prove it."

If her surprise hadn't been so genuine, it would have been comical. She studied him for a moment, then relaxed. And he was forgiven. Grabbing her jacket on her way by, she reached for the doorknob.

"Hey, Sky?"

She glanced at him over her shoulder. "Yes?"

"Alisha's mother. I mean, she and I…" His voice trailed away uncharacteristically.

"Yes?"

"Kelly's my friend." A friend he happened to want to take to bed very badly.

All grown up now, his former bratty kid sister winked as if she knew. "Don't worry. My lips are sealed."

He believed her. She was a Colton, after all. And a Colton was nothing if not as good as her word.

Grey continued to feed Alisha after Sky left. The baby stared up at him. He thought about his great-grandfather's prophecy regarding gray wolves hiding from the truth, and about his sister's opinion of his personality. Neither were particularly complimentary.

Alisha didn't seem the least concerned. She continued to drain the milk from the bottle, looking at him the entire time, as if mesmerized and totally enamored. In reality, it was the other way around. She was so darn small, so darn perfect. He could see Kelly in her features, in the shape of her eyes, the color of her hair. Even her hands were like her mother's. "You look like your mother. Of course, I've never met your father."

Alisha grunted as he placed her to his shoulder. Grey grinned.

"Tell me the truth," he said, patting her tiny back. "Your mother doesn't have any skeletons in her closet, does she?"

Her answer was a very loud, very hardy burp.

He gave her the rest of the bottle. After that, he was so busy seeing to her every need, he didn't have time to give his great-grandfather's prophecy or his sister's comment about skeletons more than a passing thought.

Chapter Seven

Kelly's eyes fluttered open, then slowly drifted shut again. She stretched a foot languidly, and sighed. Hmm. She'd been dreaming.

She opened her eyes.

She'd been dreaming, therefore, she must have been sleeping. She didn't often sleep when it was light outside. She turned her face toward the window.

It was *light* outside.

She jerked to a sitting position, her first thought, Alisha. She listened intently. Why wasn't her baby crying for her next feeding? And then it dawned on Kelly. Alisha was with Grey.

Trying to shake off the fuzziness left over from her catnap, Kelly swung her feet off the bed and glanced at the clock. She looked again. She looked a total of three times, and she still didn't believe her eyes. It was six o'clock? In the evening? Impossible. Catnaps did not last four hours.

It was six o'clock on her watch, too.

She'd only had a bottle prepared for one feeding. Alisha liked to eat every two or three hours. Surely, she was hungry.

Kelly was at her bedroom door when she heard Alisha fussing. She followed the sound to the living room, where she saw Alisha's little head bouncing gently from the other side of Grey's broad shoulder. He was walking Alisha, jiggling her, patting her narrow back. The baby was having none of it, of course, squirming and complaining.

Grey turned when he reached the far end of the room, stopping the moment he saw Kelly standing in the doorway. Something joyful and uncustomary flooded through her at the expression on his face.

She hurried toward them, reaching for the baby. "When did you get back?"

"Three hours ago."

Kelly's house was small, and yet she hadn't heard a single sound. "I must have been more tired than I thought."

"Alisha didn't decide to cry until now."

"I take it she went through all the milk I sent with you?"

"She polished off the last drop two and a half hours ago." He spoke without moving away. Kelly had to tip her head back in order to look into his eyes. "And I've discovered that the taste of water makes her mad," he added.

There was affection in his voice, and heat in his eyes. Kelly melted a little, that sensation she'd felt moments ago spreading.

Alisha was crying with gusto now. Finally breaking eye contact, Kelly said, "Excuse us."

She whisked the baby away to her bedroom where

she hurriedly unbuttoned her shirt and unfastened the special closure on her bra. Settling herself on the edge of the bed, she smoothed her hand over her baby's wispy hair, touching a finger to that perfect, soft little cheek. Kelly had slept for four blessed hours. Now that the fuzziness was leaving her brain, she felt marvelous, rested, ready to take on the world. And yet her heart beat a heavy rhythm, and had been since she'd seen the way Grey had held Alisha in his big, capable hands.

Forget male movie stars and candlelight. Kelly had just discovered that the surest way to fog up a woman's mind was to be gentle to her child. It was true. Heat had settled along the top of her heart, causing it to teeter precariously on her breastbone. Any second now it was going to tip over and slide into her stomach. It almost felt like…

Love. Soft-touched thoughts shaped her smile. Catching sight of her reflection in the mirror, she reeled in those wayward notions and sat up straighter.

She'd been down this road before, falling in love too easily. It was too soon. She had a daughter now. She had a future to make, a life to build. For Alisha's sake, she had to be strong. Next time, if there was a next time, she absolutely and honestly had to be sure. That reminded her of something Grey had said earlier, something about how honesty was in short supply these days.

Grey Colton was tall, dark and handsome, and righteous, and, okay, he was a little domineering. Above all else, he was honest. And she…

She swallowed. Kelly was honest most of the time. She was! Except for a rare white lie she told only when it was necessary to keep from hurting a friend's feelings, she didn't lie.

What about lies of omission? her conscience nagged.

Her ex-husband's image flitted into her mind. Frankie DeMarco had hair five shades of brown. He was medium built, muscular, drop-dead gorgeous. Although he knew it, he handled it pretty well. It was the other things he handled that she hadn't been able to tolerate. He'd probably loved her in the beginning. Even in the end, they'd parted friends. In her defense, she'd *tried* to do the right thing. That whole situation was fraught with extenuating circumstances.

Could she have handled the situation with Frankie differently?

She looked at Alisha, and knew she'd done the right thing for her baby. She always tried to do the right thing. Sometimes, right and wrong weren't cut-and dried, black or white.

Looking at the gift she'd bought for Grey that morning, she thought about everything he had done for her and Alisha. She wanted him to have the small token. Then and there, she also knew, without a doubt, that she was in no position to give him more than this. And no matter what she thought she felt when she'd seen him holding Alisha a few minutes ago, she couldn't give him her heart.

She continued feeding Alisha. It was good she'd had this little talk with herself. She hadn't fallen in love with Grey. Yet. Now all she had to do was make sure she kept it that way.

What a relief!

There was nothing different about her heart. She was just rested, that was all. It was amazing what a good long nap could do for a woman. She had Grey to thank for that. She had Grey to thank for a lot of things. Which brought her to call, "Did my daughter listen to those theories you mentioned, Grey?"

"What?" he called back.

After everything they'd been through, talking to him from a different room seemed silly. Slipping a lightweight baby blanket over the part of her breast not covered by her pale-blue blouse, she reached for the package, and meandered out to the living room, talking as she went. "I was just making conversation."

Grey started to rise.

She smiled. "Don't get up." He settled back down as she lowered into the rocking chair nearby. Cradling Alisha beneath the blanket, she placed the package on the table, and gently set the rocking chair in motion. "What have you and Alisha been doing for the past four hours?"

His black knit shirt was open at the neck. She couldn't help but notice that his throat convulsed slightly, as if he was trying to clear it in order to speak.

"Does this bother you?" she asked.

Bother? Forcing a nonchalance he didn't necessarily feel, Grey shook his head. Kelly's hair was mussed, a line on her cheek where she'd rested her face on her pillow. He'd passed bothered a while ago, but it wasn't her fault. She was feeding her baby. There was nothing sexual about that. In fact, it was the most nonsexual thing in the world. It was maternal, and that was beautiful.

His gaze lingered at the very edge of the narrow ridge of her collarbone visible above the blanket.

Logically he knew there was no reason for his imagination to return, time and again, to that creamy patch of skin. Trouble was, his imagination wasn't interested in logic.

The rocking chair creaked. This time she was the one getting up.

"Where are you going?" he asked.

"I'm embarrassing you. I'll finish feeding her in my room."

He reached a hand to her, stopping her progress before she could pass. "Embarrassment isn't what's ailing me, Kelly."

Kelly felt her eyes grow round as understanding dawned. Grey wanted her. That wouldn't have been a problem, except she felt an answering stir of desire in the pit of her stomach. Alisha smacked her lips, drawing Grey's gaze. Kelly watched as he glanced at the outline of the baby beneath the blanket. Slowly, he raised his gaze to hers. The entire house grew silent; the air thickened. He'd done it all with one long, heated, suggestive glance.

She'd told herself she wasn't going to fall in love with him. That was going to be easier said than done. "Grey."

"Kelly," he said at the same time.

He leaned forward, earnest and intense and masculine. Her mouth went dry. "I have a newborn baby."

"Yes, I know." His hand gentled on her arm. With his other hand, he gestured to the wrapped package she'd placed on the far table. "Is that for me?"

"It's from Alisha."

"She's already been shopping?" he asked.

"It's never too soon for a woman to start shopping."

Grey studied Kelly's expression. She seemed a little dazed. After returning to the rocking chair, she launched into a topic about her sister. In essence, she was pulling away, when he wanted to draw her closer.

He could wait. He was a patient man, after all. When she'd finished relaying her latest phone call from her sister, Mariah, he said, "This must be the day for sisters. Mine paid me a visit today."

"She did? When?"

"Sky stopped by my house while you were sleeping."

"Did she see you with Alisha?"

He tugged at his black chinos, searching for a more comfortable position. "Yes."

"Did she ask a lot of questions?"

"Do bears sleep in the woods?"

"You told her the truth?"

He nodded.

And she said, "Then that couldn't have been what you argued about."

Grey went perfectly still. It was uncanny that she'd picked up on that. "Sky and I didn't argue, exactly. We don't see eye to eye on a lot of things."

"You're saying she isn't blinded by your brains and good looks?"

He surprised himself by laughing. Looking across the small room, he wondered if Kelly was aware of the smile that stole across her face at her stab of wry humor. He wondered if she had any idea what that smile of hers was doing to him.

He knew he had to slow this down or risk having her end it before it even got started. She was an attorney. In this instance she had good grounds. She had a newborn child. Physically, emotionally, it was too soon for them to become lovers.

The very idea heated him further. He had to be patient. There was patience, and then there was patience.

"What, exactly, don't you and your sister agree upon?" she asked.

"Sky doesn't think I'm capable of spontaneity." Grey thought about his sister's opinion of him. No matter what Sky said, there was nothing wrong with setting goals and following a set course. Maybe, just maybe, he'd found the woman he wanted to walk that course with him.

"Did you set her straight?" Kelly asked.

For the flash of one instant, Grey imagined having these kinds of conversations with Kelly for the next fifty or sixty years. *Patience.* "When Sky's in one of her know-it-all moods, it isn't easy to set her straight about anything."

"My, you two are opposites."

Grey chuckled for the second time in as many minutes, a rarity for him. He felt like a kid with his nose pressed to a toy-store window five minutes before closing time. He couldn't rush Kelly. He wanted to rush her plenty.

Grey had some planning to do.

The chair creaked slightly as she rocked, and Alisha made her little baby sounds underneath the lightweight blanket. Grey didn't remember much about the rest of the conversation. After Kelly brought the baby to her shoulder and kissed that downy head, he stood. "I'll leave the two of you to the rest of the feeding."

"Really?" Kelly asked.

"Have you ever known me to lie?"

A change he didn't understand came over her face. Stopping near the rocking chair, he said, "May I?"

She nodded, and he reached for the wrapped package. Although he was curious to see what Kelly had chosen for him, he decided to open it later. Hooking his jacket on one finger, he headed for the front door.

"Grey?"

He looked back at her. Her auburn hair hung long and loose around her shoulders. Her eyes were the color of spring moss, her lips full, the outline of the upper swell of her breast visible through the blanket.

He didn't *want* to leave. This wasn't simply a case of him wanting a woman. It wasn't simple, at all. In the past, he'd used the straightforward approach when pursuing a woman. Kelly wasn't like any other woman he'd ever dated. So of course, pursuing her was going to be different.

What did his brother, Billy, the self-proclaimed black sheep of the family, call it? Covert and tactical pursuit. Billy had been bragging because he'd been involved in the hostage situation that had taken place during the Colton family reunion a few months ago. Grey preferred to leave the bragging to the other Coltons. That didn't mean he couldn't develop a tactical plan of his own. He was developing one already: advance, circle, retreat.

"Is something wrong?" she asked.

"Not at all."

She looked at him for a long time. Grey had never appreciated the Comanche wisdom and patience that had been passed on to him from his great-grandfather more than at that moment, for it allowed him to stand his ground and hold her gaze.

Advance, circle, retreat.

"Thank you," she said.

He wasn't certain what she was thanking him for. Since he would have been hard-pressed to smile, he simply said, "You're welcome." Holding up the package, he added, "Thank you."

He sauntered out to his shiny black SUV, climbed behind the wheel and tossed the package to the empty passenger seat. Patiently, he backed from her driveway and headed for his house across town.

He looked at the package a dozen times before he'd made it halfway. Pulling to a stop at a red light, he strummed his fingers on the steering wheel. And then he gave up all pretense of being a patient man.

He tore into the bright-yellow paper, then lifted the lid. Shaking the gift from the tissue paper, he could only stare. He fumbled for the note, read it and shook his head. But he was smiling when the light turned green.

Sparrows flitted from the trees to the window ledges of the county courthouse as Kelly parked her car near the big old building. The calendar said it was spring, and had been for well over a week.

She hadn't heard from Grey in more than a week. Ten days. Which was fine, of course. She was a little surprised, was all. She wondered if he liked the gift. You would think a judge would know enough about etiquette to send a note or call.

He'd done neither. Not that it mattered. After everything he'd done for her and Alisha, he didn't owe her a thing. A note would have been nice, but not necessary.

Smoothing a wrinkle from her navy skirt, she

checked her hair in the mirror and reached for her briefcase. Everything was in order: her appearance, her notes for this case, her life.

Opening the door, she got out, pushing the lock button in the process. She was to meet her boss's client inside the courthouse in five minutes. Since Cecil Walker was out with the flu, she was filling in. All she had to do was represent the firm and ask Grey for an extension. Strike that. All she had to do was ask *Judge Colton* for an extension.

She gave the car door a push, then grabbed for it. She stopped it from closing with a second to spare. Reaching inside, she retrieved her keys from the ignition.

That had been a close one.

Starting toward the steps, she reminded herself that she'd represented clients dozens of times. She wasn't nervous about that. She wasn't nervous about anything. Alisha was with a competent sitter, and Kelly had prepared the proper documents which she would turn over to Judge Colton.

Why hadn't Grey called?

She stubbed her toe on the first step. Hobbling to the top, she wondered if perhaps the inexpensive gift had offended him.

He didn't strike her as the kind of man that offended easily. He'd as much as told her he wanted her, physically at least. And she was pretty sure he liked her. And yet he hadn't called. It was better this way. It was easier, and much less risky to her heart.

Why oh why oh why hadn't he called?

One of her father's old sayings flitted through her mind. *Kelly, I swear you would complain if you were hung with a new rope.*

Kelly shuddered as she strode toward her client, who was waiting inside the door. That was simply not a good saying for an attorney to be thinking about moments before bringing a defendant face-to-face with the judge.

She shook hands with the client and exchanged pleasantries. Thankfully, she'd inherited a bit of ease and eloquence from her mother's side of the family. "Ready?" she asked.

Clive Harris nodded, but she could tell he was nervous. He needn't be. He had a rock-solid alibi and couldn't have been involved in an Internet-related computer scam. A painter—of houses—Clive didn't even own a computer. Kelly suspected that his ex-girlfriend was trying to get even with him for ending the relationship.

"Don't worry," she said quietly. "Judge Colton is fair."

They entered the courtroom and took the appropriate seats.

The bailiff called, "All rise!"

The door to the judge's chambers opened, and Grey entered the room, tall, lean and rugged, even in that loose black robe. Something that felt suspiciously like her heart floated up to Kelly's throat.

The youngest judge in the history of Comanche County looked around, taking stock of his courtroom with an all-encompassing glance. The last time Kelly had come so close to swooning was the summer after eighth grade when she and her sister had sneaked out to a New Kids on the Block concert. She'd practiced writing Mrs. Kelly Knight for weeks after that. Of course, she'd had nothing else to do, because she and

Mariah had both been grounded for life. Or so it had seemed.

Kelly shook her head to clear it, relieved to discover that her lapse hadn't lasted longer than a few seconds. Her professionalism took over. She sat up straight, answered the appropriate questions and procured the appropriate signatures on the appropriate forms. The judge was his normal, straightforward, well-spoken, cool, calm-and-collected self. Not once did Kelly's gaze linger on him longer than was appropriate.

He granted her client his extension, then pounded his gavel. He glanced around the courtroom again. When his gaze reached her, he left it there for a moment, just a moment longer than he'd left it on anyone else in the room.

"All rise!" the bailiff called.

Kelly must have risen to her feet along with everyone else. She was standing. It required careful attention to keep her breathing normal and her knees locked.

The next time she looked, Grey had left the room.

What in the world was happening to her? She gathered up her papers, exchanged a few words with the client, then left the courtroom on shaky legs. Had she imagined the unfathomable look in Grey's dark eyes?

She hadn't imagined how close she'd come to a full, female meltdown. She was overreacting. He hadn't even called.

Almost completely back in control of her sensibilities, she called goodbye to a fellow attorney and headed for the exit.

"Ms. Madison?"

Kelly turned on her sturdy navy heels.

A middle-aged clerk strode briskly toward her, and in a quiet voice, said, ''Judge Colton would like a moment of your time.''

Kelly swallowed. ''Did he say why?''

The woman shrugged kindly. ''I'm sure it's just a matter of crossing a t or dotting an i. This way.''

Kelly knew the way.

There were two entries into Judge Colton's chambers. The clerk led Kelly to the door off the corridor. She knocked briskly, then scurried away, leaving Kelly to answer Grey's ''Yes?''

Clutching her briefcase so tightly she worried for the integral strength of the plastic handle, as well as the bones in her hand, Kelly walked in.

Chapter Eight

Kelly stared at the gold nameplate on the door where she stood gripping the doorknob. Taking a deep breath, she said, "You wanted to see me?"

Grey was bent over the sink on the other side of the room. He looked up just long enough to say, "Would you close the door, please?"

He returned his attention to the faucet. And she closed the door.

The room wasn't well lit. And other than the occasional *thwunk* of the wrench in Grey's hand, it was quiet. Kelly was the quietest of all. She hung back, timidity warring with curiosity. It wasn't every day a person saw a judge wielding a wrench.

He placed the tool next to the sink as if admitting defeat. "This faucet has been dripping for months. I think I just made it worse."

Her father was a plumber. She was pretty sure Grey was using the wrong tool. Uncertain why he'd sent for her, she decided not to mention it.

He'd unzipped his robe, and was dressed all in black underneath it. He looked so good in black. She closed her eyes, girding herself with resolve.

He wiped his hands on a paper towel, slowly, meticulously, thoroughly. "Thank you for the shirt."

She looked up at him, surprised by the referral to the gift she'd given him ten days ago. He was looking directly into her eyes. She swallowed, her resolve fading. "It fits?"

"Perfectly."

"Oh. Good. You're welcome." And then, because she couldn't think of anything else to say, and a silence had developed between them again, she added, "It was so you."

They shared a smile, hers big, his small, because they both knew that the brightly colored, rayon, sales-bin Hawaiian-print shirt was the most unlike-him shirt in the world, unless she counted the sleeveless, denim numbers some of the musicians were wearing these days.

"To tell you the truth," she said, "I had intended to pick up a white dress shirt to replace the one you wrapped Alisha in right after she was born, but I wasn't sure about neck sizes and sleeve length, and then I saw the Hawaiian-print shirt, and I couldn't resist." She was rambling; she couldn't help it. "Not that I'm making light of what you did. I'm still completely grateful."

"Kelly?"

She stopped fidgeting with the pearly button on her jacket and shut up. Had he moved closer? Or had she?

"Am I making you nervous?" he asked.

It was him. He'd moved closer.

"Of course not!" That was when she knew. They'd

both moved closer, as if propelled by a force greater than either of them. She swallowed. "Well. Maybe I am a little nervous. It's awfully dark in here."

"There's a glitch in the wiring. Something to do with the new construction. Unfortunately, my office is on an inside corridor, therefore there's no window. Judges aren't encouraged to do a lot of daydreaming."

Kelly had no idea how to respond to that. She didn't think it was wise to continue in that vein, lest they get into the particulars about other daydreams, night dreams or fantasies, especially fantasies. Finally, she settled for saying, "Norma said you wanted to see me."

He refastened his robe, slowly drawing the zipper all the way up the front. Kelly couldn't seem to look away.

"Would you care to have dinner with me this weekend?" he asked.

"Dinner?"

"Before you agree, I must warn you that the invitation is for a home-cooked dinner at my parents' home."

"Your parents?" When had she become a parrot? "Your mother still wants to meet Alisha?"

"My mother was a schoolteacher for thirty-six years. She never forgets anything, least of all a promise."

"Well, of course. By all means. I mean, I'd love to have your mother meet Alisha. I'm surprised, that's all. I thought... I mean, when you didn't call, I assumed..."

She closed her mouth and her eyes. When she opened them, her eyes, that is, Grey was moving steadily closer. She knew, because she backed up just as steadily, stopping only when she backed squarely into his desk.

Fleetingly, she wondered what had happened to her briefcase. She didn't remember dropping it, so she must have set it down. Without it, she didn't know where to put her hands. On a pair of broad shoulders came to mind.

"I'm not much for talking on the phone," he said.

Now that she thought about it, she'd noticed. She guessed that explained why he never called before coming over.

"How is Alisha, by the way?"

"She's wonderful. She stopped waking up just to cry in the middle of the night. She weighs eight pounds now." Kelly's voice sounded breathless in her own ears. There was good reason for that. Grey had stopped a matter of inches away from her, standing so close she could feel the heat emanating off his chest.

"You're at work," she said.

"Yes, I know."

"We're both at work." She wished she had the presence of mind to give herself a swift mental kick. Any second now, she was going to tell him the sky was blue and his eyes were brown.

His eyes were brown, and fathomless, and very close to hers. And they were getting closer all the time.

"Grey."

This time, he remained silent. And she knew there was no sense telling him they could only be friends. He knew better, and so did she. In the very least, they needed to set up some boundaries for their relationship. Gulp. If that was what this was.

Is that what this was? She wet her lips, swallowed the nerves in her throat. "What would you say is happening between us?"

"To borrow an eloquent phrase from my twin brothers, I'd say we have the hots for each other."

"Oh, my. Oh dear. But, um. I guess. That is."

"Yes?" He cocked one eyebrow. She'd always wondered how men did that.

"Actually, that's just the beginning. I like you, Kelly."

He did? She swallowed again. "We must remain professional, therefore, this must remain…"

"Clandestine?" he asked.

"Platonic," she said at the same time.

"Ever notice how often we speak at the same time?" he asked.

She nodded.

And he said, "I prefer my words better."

"You would." She brought both her hands up, and dropped her face into them.

Slowly, gently, Grey wrapped his fingers around her wrists and drew her hands away from her face. Kelly Madison had the greenest, the deepest, most captivating eyes. She looked back at him, dazed. Grey didn't blame her. In a sense, he'd ambushed her. She'd certainly had no warning, while he'd had ten days to plan his strategy. Advance. Circle. Retreat.

His request that she come to his chambers had been the advance. Everything after that was, in effect, circling. Now, for the retreat. It was his least favorite tactical maneuver. He took a backward step. "I have a docket full of cases."

Her mouth moved, but no sound came.

"My father gets indigestion if he eats after seven, so why don't I pick you and Alisha up around six-thirty?"

Still looking slightly dazed, Kelly nodded. "Six-thirty." Yes, that proved it. She was a parrot. "What day?"

"Saturday."

"Of course," she said. "I'll see you then."

Grey retrieved her briefcase, handed it to her, then walked out one door. Looking around dazedly, Kelly exited via the other one.

"Do you feel like the chauffeur?" Kelly asked, seated next to Alisha in the back seat of what she called Grey's tank. For the life of her, she didn't know why he found that description of his SUV so amusing.

"I don't mind. It's the safest place for Alisha, right?"

Kelly sighed. She couldn't see Grey's facial expression from back here, but his voice was clear and sincere.

He'd picked them up right on time five minutes ago. Now they were driving through a section of town Kelly had only glimpsed until now. Alisha was looking around, sucking noisily on a bright-yellow pacifier. Before she'd had her baby, Kelly had adamantly insisted that her child would never have a pacifier. Buying one and offering it to her child was the third rule Kelly had broken. And Alisha was only three weeks old. Starting a love relationship with Grey was the first, second, and fourth.

Alisha seemed perfectly content with the situation. Kelly was on dangerous, exciting, terrifying ground.

"Okay," she said, referring to the information Grey had relayed a few minutes ago. "Amber, Sophie, Rand, Emily, Joe and Meredith are some of the California Coltons."

"That's right."

"And the Oklahoma Coltons didn't know they existed until recently."

"Neither branch knew of the other."

"The California Coltons are rich," Kelly said.

"Very," he said.

He'd told her how the two branches had decided to meet in Georgetown at Christmas for a monumental family reunion that had culminated at Grey's younger brother's wedding on Christmas Eve. It sounded to Kelly as though it had turned out to be quite a reunion, too, complete with a SWAT team and a hostage situation.

"You're rich, too." She was referring to the ten million dollars Grey had told her the family had discovered in a trust fund after their grandmother had died.

"On a much smaller scale, yes, although we never knew that, either."

She smoothed her hand over the fabric of her brown trousers. She'd chosen the slacks and sandals for comfort, the green knit top because the buttons down the front made feeding Alisha easier. The fact that it matched her eyes was a coincidence. "I don't think you should be telling people this," she said.

"Why?"

She stared at the trees and houses going by outside

the window. "Haven't you ever heard of gold diggers?"

He chuckled.

"It isn't funny. *I* could be a gold digger for all you know."

"You're not."

His gaze met hers through the rearview mirror. His eyes were warm, his look one of faint amusement. She melted a little inside. "You sound awfully sure."

"You're sunny and outgoing. You work pro bono half the time. You believe in people nobody else believes in. But you don't stop there. You *befriend* them."

Kelly melted a little more. If they didn't get there soon, she was going to fall all the way in love before dinner.

As luck would have it, he pulled into his parents' driveway before that happened. "Okay," she said, studying the inviting lines of the old white house where Grey had spent his formative years. "I believe every word you've said about your family. And I don't want to hear any more talk about how you think my family is a little weird."

Alice and Tom Colton heard their eldest son's laughter from the front porch. They looked at each other, eyebrows raised. But neither spoke as they started down the steps to greet their company.

Dinner was delicious. Alice Colton was a good cook, Tom Colton a good conversationalist. Unfortunately, he hadn't directed any of the conversation to his wife. Kelly noticed that immediately.

Both of Grey's parents had made a fuss over Alisha. Alice had wiped away a tear, and Tom had slapped his eldest son on the back.

Alice Colton had gray hair, no-nonsense gray eyes and a contagious smile. Shorter than Kelly, her hands were steady, her touch gentle but firm. Kelly could only imagine how many children she'd nurtured throughout her years as an elementary-school teacher. And then there were the six children she'd reared.

Kelly had chosen her daughter's name well.

Tom Colton wasn't quite as tall as his son. At sixty-one, he still had most of his hair, and was openly proud of it. He did most of the talking.

Alisha napped through the entire meal. The conversation was relaxed, and sprinkled with the names of Grey's siblings, their spouses and future spouses. Although Kelly sensed a certain underlying tension between Tom and Alice, she hadn't put her finger on the cause. But she would, if she kept them talking long enough.

Too full to accept a second helping of anything, Kelly looked at Alice and said, "Everything was delicious. Truly." She smiled at Tom next. "And I had no idea just how many heroes there were in the Colton clan."

Tom buttered his roll. "I've always felt it's far more impressive when others discover our good qualities without our help."

Alice rolled her eyes and pursed her lips. She was energetic, expressive. Tom was droll. Kelly liked them both a great deal. She met Grey's gaze across the table. His parents weren't the only ones she liked a great deal.

Tom must have noticed the way his son was looking at Kelly. Whether it was an inborn quality, or one

that had been honed while a career army man or later
when he'd been a consultant in security work, he began asking Kelly questions. She answered his queries
about her childhood easily and humorously. She was
so relaxed she never saw the question about Alisha's
father coming.

"Alisha's father?" she asked, her parroting problem back, the hand holding her fork frozen inches
above her untouched slice of apple pie.

"Yes," Tom said around his own bite of pie.

Alice shot her husband a quelling glare.

"What?" Tom asked, defensive. "Every kid has
one, right?"

"Alisha has a father, of course," Kelly said quietly, finding it easier to look at Tom than at Grey.
"He isn't in the picture."

"Why the hell isn't he?" Tom asked.

"Tom!" Alice reprimanded.

"What?"

"Some things are personal."

"It's all right," Kelly said, trying to diffuse the
tension. "Really. Frankie just isn't what you would
call father material."

"It's his loss," Tom said, glancing at the baby.

Alice started to clear up. Kelly looked at Grey, and
found him staring at her, as if trying to understand
something. She wavered him a woman-soft smile,
then rose to help Alice.

"Grey," Tom said, "tell your mother the meal was
delicious, and I'll be outside working on the car."

Grey eyed the door leading to the kitchen, his father, and then Kelly. There was more to the tension
in the air than his parents' ongoing feud. Grey said,
"Is something wrong with the car, Dad?"

Tom Colton shrugged. ''A journey of a thousand miles always seems to begin with a broken fan belt and a flat tire.''

Grey dropped his napkin next to his plate. ''Are you taking a trip?''

''Who knows.'' Which probably meant that he was going to tinker out in the driveway because things were so strained inside.

His mother and Kelly both disappeared into the kitchen. Alisha was still sleeping on the buffet in the contraption Kelly called a baby carrier. Grey took his and his father's plates into the kitchen. After his mother shooed him out again, he saw no reason not to follow his father outside. Once there, his dad popped the release and lifted the hood on the old family coupe.

''So Kelly's the one.''

''I didn't know it was that obvious.''

Tom Colton never beat around the bush. Today was no exception. ''Trouble?'' he asked.

Grey eyed the window where he could see two heads at the kitchen sink. ''It's too early to tell,'' he answered. There was something about the way Kelly had dodged those questions about Alisha's father.

''I have two theories about how to deal with women,'' Tom said.

He had Grey's undivided attention.

Bending over the engine, his father fiddled with something and muttered, ''Both fail, of course.''

With a shake of his head, Grey thought it was no wonder his mother wasn't speaking to this man.

In the kitchen, Alice washed a plate and handed it to Kelly to dry. ''Don't mind Grey's father. He sometimes asks about things that aren't any of his business."

"It's all right," Kelly said. She'd carried Alisha, baby seat and all, into the kitchen. The baby was awake now, evidently fascinated with the light fixture hanging from the ceiling above the kitchen table.

"In that case," Alice said, smiling at the baby, "I just have to say that I find it amazing and unfathomable how any man could help but get all wrapped around this little one's finger."

Kelly stared at the light fixture, too, lost in thought. Even though Alice had changed the subject, the niggling voice in the back of Kelly's mind refused to go away.

Eventually, Alice's voice drew Kelly's attention. The older woman was peering out the window. "Look at them. It never ceases to amaze me how good-looking my men are."

Kelly nodded, although she wasn't really amazed. The fact that Grey Colton was attractive was widely accepted in Comanche County. And now that she'd met Tom and Alice, she knew where Grey had come by his looks.

"Luckily," Alice said, as if reading Kelly's mind, "Grey isn't as bullheaded as his father."

Kelly dried another dish. "No offense, but are you sure about that?"

Alice almost smiled. "Lord, yes, I'm sure. It's like Eleanor Roosevelt said. No one can make you feel inferior without your permission."

She was staring out the window again, so Kelly said, "Is that what this is about? Is Mr. Colton making you feel inferior?"

"Tom? Heavens no. He knows better."

"Then what is it that's driving you so crazy?"

Just like that, Alisha grew bored with the light fixture and started to fuss. "May I?" Alice asked. At Kelly's nod, she dried her hands on a faded kitchen towel and reached for the baby dressed all in yellow. "I didn't say he was driving me crazy."

Kelly had almost given up all hope that Alice was going to continue, when the older woman said, "He's like a cat."

Kelly looked up from the bowl she was drying. "I beg your pardon?"

"He's always underfoot. He follows me from room to room without making a sound. I'm sure it was a great asset in his security-consulting work all these years, but now, I turn around, and there he is. We used to have the most heated and interesting conversations." Alice stroked Alisha's little head, inhaling the baby scent that couldn't be bottled. "He had strong opinions, but he used to save them for the important issues, like drunk driving, politics, the death penalty and recycling."

Kelly smiled at that last one.

"I loved hearing what he had to say." Alice patted Alisha's back. "I loved arguing with him even more."

"He doesn't talk about the important issues anymore?"

Alice shook her head sadly.

"What do the two of you talk about?" Kelly asked.

"Not much." Alice fiddled with the baby's blanket. "Hardly anything," she added so quietly Kelly almost didn't hear.

"Yet he follows you around?"

Alice sighed. "Last week I literally tripped over

him after I finished making the bed. It was the final straw.''

Kelly thought it would be wise not to mention that Grey had told her that his parents were sleeping in separate rooms these days. ''What did Mr. Colton— Tom,'' she amended at the expression that settled over the former schoolteacher's face, ''what did Tom do?''

Alice sat down at the table. Turning watery gray eyes to Kelly, she hugged Alisha closer and said, ''Do you really want to hear this?''

''Sometime, ask Grey about my parents. All families have their idiosyncrasies. Last week, I bailed a very angry and misunderstood client out of jail. I can honestly say that I've more than likely heard it all.''

Alice sighed. Lowering her voice an octave in order to better mimic her husband, Grey's mother continued. '''Alice,' he said, 'I couldn't help noticing that you didn't pull the sheet and blankets as tight as you should have.'''

''Oh, dear,'' Kelly said.

Alice nodded, her face pretty, her eyes sad. She shook herself slightly. ''It seems that when Tom was in the army, they taught him how to make a bed so tight you could bounce a quarter off it.''

''Oh dear,'' Kelly said again, her empathy growing. ''And what did you do?''

''I asked him if he had a quarter.''

Kelly waited, breath bated.

''He did, of course. The man is nothing if not prepared.''

''And?'' Kelly asked.

''I told him to give it a whirl.''

Alice looked Kelly in the eye. "The quarter landed in the center of the bed with barely a sound."

"It didn't bounce?"

Alice shook her head. "Lord, no. I knew it wouldn't. Who needs to make a quarter bounce on a bed? Tom turned to me, all know-it-all like. And I told him I hoped he and his quarter were very happy together in our bed from now on."

So that explained the separate beds, Kelly thought.

"And that was the last we spoke on the subject."

It seemed to Kelly that that was the last they'd spoken on any subject. The men came in. Alisha wanted to eat. By the time Kelly had finished feeding the baby, Grey was making noises about leaving.

Grey's mother surprised Kelly by hugging her. Tom hung back. Kelly noticed that Grey was quiet, too. During the drive back to her place, she said, "Is something wrong, Grey?"

"It's worse than I thought."

"What is?"

"My parents. Sky was right. My father's miserable."

His mother was miserable, too, but Kelly figured Grey already knew that. "It isn't as serious as you might think."

He pulled to a stop at a red light then glanced over his shoulder at her. "You spent a half hour alone with my mother and you know what's tearing apart their marriage?"

"Your father told your mother how to make the bed."

"He what?" And then, "I don't see how that—"

"She's been making beds fine for a long time."

"This has to do with making beds?" he asked, obviously perplexed.

"Of course not."

"But you just said."

"The light's green, Grey."

He started through the intersection.

Kelly continued. "Now that he's retired, your father's bored. And underfoot. He needs a project. Actually, they both do."

He was silently thoughtful. Finally, he said, "But they're retired. This is supposed to be the time of their lives."

"It still can be. But they need a project. Didn't you tell me the Oklahoma Coltons were looking for a way to put that ten million dollars to good use?"

Grey nodded.

"Who better than a retired schoolteacher and a retired security consultant slash army man to head up a big, charitable project? I don't know how far ten million dollars would go, but it certainly seems like they should be able to find a good use for it."

"You mean start a foundation of some sort? I wonder what it would take to get if off the ground. But you're right! Who better than my mother and father to do it? They could head it up. A charity. Something that would put that money and their talents to good use. Something for kids, maybe. I'll run the idea by Sky, and Billy, and Jesse." He pulled into her driveway. Opening the door for her, he said, "You're brilliant, and good to your soul, and gorgeous."

She was trying to get Alisha out of the car, but he swooped closer and kissed Kelly before she'd unfastened the seat belt. The kiss was long, and slow, and deep. By the time it ended, the blood pounding through Kelly's ears nearly obliterated the sounds the kids were making playing down the block.

"I've been wanting to do that all night," he said.

It was Grey who took Alisha, cradling the baby, infant car seat and all, in his arms. Kelly followed them to the house, that niggling doubt hazy but persistent around the edges in the back of her mind. She needed to talk to Grey. She wanted another kiss. What was a woman to do?

Kelly didn't get a chance to do any talking or kissing during the next hour. Grey had called his brother a little while ago. Now, at nearly ten o'clock, Kelly was drawing a blanket over her baby in the crib in the nursery. Alisha was sound asleep, her arms bent at the elbows, her hands on either side of her head. Her light-brown hair stuck out in little tufts at her crown and above her ears. She had the most perfect ears. Her eyelashes were already curly where they rested above her cheeks, her nose unbelievably tiny and pug, her mouth like a perfect bow, her lips sucking now and then, as if she was dreaming about eating.

Kelly smiled at the thought. Her child had a strong will. It was up to Kelly to mold this beautiful baby into the kind of woman who would reach her full potential. The responsibility was mind-boggling. Kelly could think of nothing in the world that would have more meaning than raising her child. But she wasn't only *her* child.

That niggling doubt was back. Kelly had to talk to Grey.

Leaning down, she pressed a feather-soft kiss on Alisha's forehead, checked the blankets one more time, switched on the star-shaped night-light, then tip-toed from the room.

She needed to talk to Grey when her head was clear. To that end, she'd better not let him kiss her until *after* the conversation. She couldn't help but wonder if he would still want to kiss her then. It was an unsettling thought. But she couldn't let it keep her from what she had to do.

Although Grey was still on the phone in the living room, his eyes warmed at least ten degrees the moment he looked at her. He shrugged, pointed to his watch, indicating that he'd try to put an end to the call momentarily, then moved his fingers like a mouth opening and closing over and over.

Kelly smiled in spite of herself. Settling in the corner of the sofa, she drew her legs up, resting her arms on bent knees. Although it wasn't easy to determine everything that was being said when she only heard one side of the conversation, Kelly could tell that Grey's brother liked the idea Grey had presented. Grey had insinuated that Billy liked to talk; Grey appeared to be enjoying it. The Colton clan was a close-knit family. And close-knit families could talk up a blue streak. Kelly aimed the remote at the television.

"Actually," Grey said, his voice deep and quiet and terribly masculine, "I can't take the credit."

Feeling his eyes on her, Kelly looked up from the television program she was pretending to watch. Something warm and delicious passed between their gazes. She had to remind herself to breathe. While she was at it, she reminded herself that it was very important that she speak with him. And she had to do it before he kissed her.

He hung up the phone, finally. Turning, all shoulders and brawn, he moved with purpose, not haste. Kelly tried her darnedest not to drool.

"That was Billy."

Yes, she'd figured as much. "Bad Boy Billy?"

He nodded. "He told me to give you a kiss for him."

She swallowed wobbly. "Grey." She held up one hand. She had to learn not to do that for it gave him the perfect opportunity to take her hand, which he did.

He lowered his lanky frame near her on the sofa. "Don't worry. It's like I told him. I'd rather kiss you for me."

Uh-oh.

He inched closer, his shoulder brushing hers, his eyes hooded, and oh, so inviting. He was making that sound he made in the back of his throat, part groan, part hum, all yearning.

Or was that coming from inside her?

Any second now he was going to kiss her. She was supposed to resist. She remembered that much.

His mouth was an inch from hers, his eyes still open. Her own vision blurred. Her heart skipped a beat, then raced in double time. Her lips parted, and she sighed. At the last second, she drew back an inch. Her back straightened, proof that she still had a backbone. The haze in her brain cleared slightly. Another news flash: She actually still had a brain.

She had control of her sensibilities, too. She proved it by placing a hand on his chest and spreading her fingers wide. Looking him in the eye, she said, "Wait, Grey. We need to talk."

Chapter Nine

The pale glow of the television fell like moonlight across the carpet in Kelly's quiet living room. Shadows pooled in corners and underneath end tables. Grey's eyes should have been in the shadows, too, but they were lit from an energy that seemed to be coming from within. Kelly's hand was still flattened along his chest, her fingers spread wide. The flesh underneath was warm, his chest muscled, his heart beating strong and steady.

"We need to talk." It sounded much more convincing this time. So far so good. "And since I can't talk, can't even think, when you kiss me, you have to promise not to. Kiss me, that is."

He stared at her for several long, searing seconds. Although it seemed to cost him, he said, "Okay. I won't kiss you. Until you want me to."

Her brain was fogging up again, because wanting had nothing to do with this.

"What is this about, Kelly?" he asked.

"My ex-husband."

"I'm listening."

Yes, he was. He was also touching her, his hand warming her skin through her slacks, where he was kneading the inside of her knee.

"His name is Frank DeMarco. He's in real estate up in Tulsa." Although he'd been between jobs the last time she'd seen him. She shook her head, reminding herself to stick to the pertinent facts.

"Do you ever talk to him?" Grey's hand was moving up her leg, a quarter of an inch at a time, kneading, circling, warming her skin and her imagination.

"No." Was that her voice? So low and shivery. She hadn't spoken to Frankie since he'd signed the divorce papers. She placed a hand over Grey's, holding it still just in case he planned to ease it on into more dangerous territory.

"Does Alisha look like him?" he asked.

"No. Well, maybe when she's screaming her head off in the middle of the night. Seriously, not even then."

He almost smiled.

Before she got lost in the heat in his eyes all over again, she forged ahead. "Frankie and I met in college at the University of Illinois. We had a class together, and actually, I had no intention of getting involved with him. I knew he wanted me, but then, Frankie wanted most girls. One day he came to me and asked if I would tutor him in business law."

"Not the brightest person, I take it?"

She swatted Grey's hand this time. "He's smart when he applies himself." He'd applied himself to pursuing her. A girl from the suburbs whose biggest adventure had been sneaking to a rock concert hadn't known what hit her.

"You must have fallen in love with him if you married him."

She didn't quite know what to make of the edge in Grey's voice. "I was young. A paltry excuse, I know. And really, I think he loved me in the beginning."

Grey sat perfectly still, listening. Finally, he said, "He hurt you."

Yes, but that wasn't what she wanted to talk about. She was moments away from revealing her secret, and she still didn't know where to begin. "Frankie DeMarco was and probably always will be the life of every party. His smile turns heads. I'm not exaggerating. His laughter is infectious. Back then I believed in fairy tales. We got married right after college graduation. It wasn't long after the wedding that I discovered he wasn't going to be my knight in shining armor."

"Did he hit you?"

"No."

"Drink?"

"Not in excess."

"What then?"

"He cheated on me." To this day, it wasn't easy to say. "He was everybody's friend, but nobody's hero. Especially not mine."

"So you filed for divorce."

That sounded very cut-and-dried. It hadn't been that easy, but yes, she'd filed for divorce, eventually, after it happened again, after she'd realized he wasn't going to change. She was in law school by then. Turns out that was his problem, or so he'd said. He was bored when she was so busy. Eventually, Kelly realized that she intimidated him. He needed a weaker woman, one who needed him no matter what he did. She wasn't that woman. Thank God. Frankie had moved to Tulsa, and it took a while for the papers to catch up with him. "It was either file for divorce or have an open marriage, and I'm just not that open-minded."

"You deserve better than that."

Now why on earth did she feel complimented? She also felt understood. The stern, though fair, judge of Comanche County understood her.

The only lamp on in the room was in the far corner. It did as little in the way of lighting the room as the television. The house was quiet, warm. Romantic. Which was silly, because there was a pacifier on the end table, a baby bottle on the floor and baby paraphernalia everywhere. It wasn't the setting that was making this romantic. It was Grey. It was how she felt about him, and how he made her feel.

He was looking at her mouth again, and she knew he wanted to kiss her. That wasn't all he wanted. It wasn't all she wanted, either. But he wouldn't kiss her, because he'd said he wouldn't. He was a man of his word, and no matter how she'd tried to slow this down, she hadn't been able to keep from falling in love with him.

But she wasn't finished. There was something else she had to tell him. "Grey, about Alisha."

"Is her last name DeMarco?" he asked.

Kelly shook her head. "Frankie and I were already divorced by the time she was born." She wasn't proud of this. She knew women who slept with their ex-husbands. She never thought she'd be one of them. Alisha had been conceived the same day they'd

signed the papers, actually. Kelly had been lonely and
Frankie had been kind and funny and his usual en-
dearing, lighthearted self. He knew the part of her that
had been young. Seeing him again had brought back
so many feelings, and one thing had led to another.
Maybe it had been habit, and what they said was true.
Old habits died hard. Or maybe it had been a mistake.
Whatever it had been, the result was the best thing
that had ever happened to Kelly.

Alisha.

"I'm glad you named her Alisha Grace Madison."

She reached a hand to Grey's face. He leaned
closer, bringing his face directly in front of hers.

"Grey, it isn't what you think. I gave her my last
name instead of Frankie's because—"

The phone rang.

They both jumped.

By the second ring, they'd both recovered enough
to look at the annoying contraption. Kelly started to
rise on the third ring.

"Leave it," Grey said.

"Nobody calls me after ten o'clock unless it's important. It's probably an emergency. It could be my
dad. He was going to the doctor this week." She put
the phone to her ear and said, "Madison residence."

Grey sat forward on Kelly's sofa. "Yes," he heard
her say. She sounded more confused than worried.

He took a deep breath and let it all out slowly.
There had been nothing about anything Kelly had told
him that had been lust arousing, and yet he'd never
wanted another woman more. He looked across the
room at her. She was speaking in hushed tones. Several tendrils of hair had slipped free of the clasp that

had held her hair off her neck. Her slacks were wrinkled, her shirt untucked.

She was beautiful.

He'd heard women complain about how long it took them to get their figure back after having a baby. Kelly's figure looked good to him. He'd always considered himself a leg man, but he rather enjoyed all aspects of a woman's body, Kelly's especially.

"Yes," she said again. "Yes, he's here."

She handed the phone to Grey.

Even with the phone in his hand, it took him a moment to comprehend that the call was for him. He put the phone to his ear. "This is Grey Colton."

"I hope I'm not interrupting anything."

"Sky? What's wrong?"

"Nothing."

"Then, what, why, how did you get this number?"

"Billy gave it to me. Geez, Grey, you're hurting my ear."

As long as he'd jumped to his feet, he paced to the far side of the room. Lowering his voice, he said, "How did Billy get Kelly's number?"

"Ever hear of caller ID? Billy said you were in a great mood. You don't sound in a good mood to me."

Grey ran a hand through his hair, thinking that was because Billy hadn't interrupted Kelly moments before she'd given him a long, searing kiss that very well could have become more. His body was still thrumming with what might have been.

"You've already talked to Billy?" he asked.

"Yes, and I think it's a fabulous idea." He heard the excitement in his sister's voice. "Hold on, Grey. I've got Jesse on the line, too. Thought he might like to get in on the plan at ground level."

Then and there, Grey accepted the fact that this was inevitable. The three Coltons talked for the next ten minutes via Sky's three-way calling, of all things. Jesse worked as a national security agent, and spent much of his time in Washington, D.C. It had been his wedding to Samantha Cosgove that had prompted that family reunion that had turned into a hostage situation last Christmas. Everything had turned out in the end. Jesse sounded good. Now that Grey thought about it, Sky did, too. They were happy. And it had to do with matters of the heart. Grey was beginning to think he might sound like Sky and Jesse one day soon.

Right now, he would settle for that kiss the phone call had interrupted. It took another ten minutes to get off the phone. After saying goodbye to Sky and Jesse, he put the phone down on the end table and started toward Kelly again, only to stop a few steps away.

Her head was turned, her knees still drawn up close to her body. Her arms were crossed over her chest, her chin resting on one hand. Her eyes were closed, her breathing even. It was too late to take up where they'd left off. Kelly was fast asleep.

Kelly felt the warmth of the throw placed gently over her. She must have been dreaming. In her dream, she heard the door open and close, too. In some far corner of her mind, she questioned that. It was the sound of an engine starting up out in her driveway that finally awakened her. Headlights flickered off the living-room wall. She threw off the blanket and ran to the window just as Grey's taillights disappeared down the street.

He was gone.

She'd fallen asleep. How could she have done that?

Until she'd had Alisha, she'd never fallen asleep unless she was in bed. The experts in the books she'd read said it was due to sleep deprivation. It was normal, they said. She thought it was awful.

She was turning away from the window when she noticed the note on the desk. She padded over and picked it up.

Have dinner with me.
Roberto's.
I'll pick you up at seven.
You choose the day.
Whatever works best for you.
Just let me know.
Grey

She stared at Grey's concise, masculine handwriting. It was legible, the words succinct, with just enough room for her input to make her smile.

She carried the note with her as she checked on Alisha. Her baby was sound asleep, perfect and precious in every way. Kelly touched her finger to her daughter's tiny hand.

"Grey's gone," she whispered. "And Mommy still hasn't told him that there's a good reason you don't have your father wrapped around your little finger."

Alisha made a humming, sleeping sound that Kelly adored. Wiping away a tear that had rolled down her own cheek, Kelly took a deep breath and read Grey's note again.

Next, she readied herself for bed. Leaving the note on her bedstand, she crawled between her sheets. She lay on her back, staring at the dark ceiling. Finally, she finished her confession. "Frank DeMarco doesn't know he has a child."

Kelly stood looking at her reflection in the full-length mirror. Grey would be here any minute.

It was Friday, the day they were going to have dinner at Roberto's. She hadn't chosen it because she was trying to put off telling him the rest of her secret, but because it was the only day Clara Jones, the mother of the boy she'd defended a few weeks ago, could watch Alisha. And no matter what complications Kelly faced, Alisha, and Alisha's well-being, remained the most important elements in Kelly's life.

It was hard to believe her baby was nearly a month old. It was harder to believe that Kelly had fallen in love in precisely that amount of time.

She turned this way and that, stepping over three other dresses she'd tried and discarded. This little black number with its rounded neckline and cap sleeves was going to have to suffice despite the fact that it pulled a little across the bodice. The others pulled worse, and in worse places. Black was a good color for a woman with a month-old baby, and the sheath style skimmed over what she'd formerly referred to as her waist.

She'd decided to leave her hair down. It felt more casual this way, but failed to ease any feelings of impending doom.

She checked her watch. Grey would be here any minute. She didn't have much time. She got busy applying mascara, blush and lipstick. She'd already prepared a bottle for Alisha. The pediatrician's number was by the phone, along with her cell phone number and the telephone number for Roberto's.

Kelly had never eaten there. She'd heard about it, though.

"We'll go when you're older," she told Alisha, who was watching from the counter next to the bathroom sink. "Like your Grandpa Madison would say, when our ship comes in."

After slipping into her black, sling-back shoes—sure-thing shoes, her sister, Mariah, called them—Kelly lifted her baby from her little carrier seat and whispered, "Wish Mommy luck."

Alisha stared at Kelly. And then her baby did something she'd been perfecting all week. She smiled. Kelly's heart turned over. "You be good for Clara. And just between you and me, I'm taking that smile as a good sign."

Kelly felt better. Perhaps the night wasn't earmarked for disaster.

Of course it wasn't. Grey was a good man. A fair man. Just because he was a judge didn't mean he judged people outside the courtroom. Look how involved he'd gotten with the plans his parents and siblings were making to put that windfall to good use. He believed in Kelly, too. He'd told her in almost those exact words.

It wasn't too late to tell him the whole truth. Once he knew, he would understand.

She hoped.

She entered her living room from the hallway the same time Grey walked through the front door.

"Wow," Clara Jones declared, closing the textbook she'd been studying. "You look amazing, Kelly."

"You took the words right out of my mouth," Grey said.

As far as Kelly was concerned, Grey looked pretty amazing, too. He stood across the room, black suit, white shirt, dark, windblown hair.

Kelly handed Alisha to Clara, then went over a few last-minute instructions while she kissed her daughter's little cheek. From there, Kelly practically floated out to Grey's car. Holding the door for her, he said, "For the record, you don't look like anybody's mother."

"Oh, Grey." Her heels put her closer to his height, her shoulder nestled comfortably a few inches below his.

"When you say my name like that, it feeds a fantasy of mine. Care to hear it?"

His voice was a deep, resonate baritone that strummed something to life inside Kelly. "Do I have a choice?"

He laughed, and she thought, *He's been doing that a lot lately.* Laughing. Everything was going to be all right.

He closed her door then hurried around to the driver's side. He didn't talk about those fantasies during the drive to the restaurant. Instead, he said, "I have a message to relay from my father. If I don't tell you right now, I won't get back to it."

Kelly understood. Boy did she understand.

"My parents are in California, meeting with our cousins, looking over a foundation called the Hope-chest Ranch. The California Coltons have been running it for years for troubled teens and unwed mothers and runaways. Often, it's these kids' last chance before life succeeds in beating them into the ground. When Mom and Dad return, they want to throw a party. And they want you to be there."

"They're in California, and they're already planning a party?"

"Across the board, Coltons are better at advancing and circling than retreating."

Kelly had no idea what he was talking about. She studied his profile. She couldn't believe she'd once thought he looked severe. His eyes were warm, his mouth made for rakish grins.

"Everyone in the family is in complete agreement, a first, by the way, about your idea."

"That's nice, Grey."

"Not a lot of people have accused me of being nice. Until lately."

Nerves fluttered in the pit of Kelly's stomach. She tamped them down and tried to concentrate on what Grey was saying.

"We aren't going to be able to do anything on such a grand scale with only ten million dollars, but Mom and Dad already have several good ideas."

"They're talking? To each other?"

"Thanks to you. If I wasn't driving, I'd kiss you."

If he wasn't driving, she would tie him up and gag him so she could get a word in edgewise.

They arrived at the restaurant with a few minutes to spare. Roberto's was a rustic, trendy restaurant in one of the oldest buildings in Black Arrow. A large, stone fireplace separated the foyer from the dining area, where waiters in black pants and bow ties carried huge trays over their shoulders.

A pretty, young hostess told them their table was almost ready, and indicated that they should have a seat at the Victorian-style sofa if they'd like. Kelly and Grey had nearly reached the cluster of sofas, when an older gentleman and his wife called to Grey.

Kelly and Grey met the older couple in the center of the small room. "Senator Fitzgerald, Mrs. Fitzgerald," Grey said. "It's good to see you."

Introductions were made. Kelly had heard of Senator Fitzgerald, but this was the first time she'd met him and his wife in person. Hadley Fitzgerald had a receding hairline, a sharp, assessing stare and a firm handshake. Beatrice, his wife, was a tall, angular woman with gray-blue eyes and a regal air. Both had genuine smiles.

The Fitzgeralds were on their way back to Oklahoma City after visiting friends over in Lawton. The four exchanged pleasantries for a few moments, and then the senator turned to Grey. "Has the man who set fire to the Comanche County Courthouse gone to trial?"

Grey said, "Not yet. His name is Kenny Randolph."

"Oh dear," Beatrice said drolly to Kelly. "Shoptalk."

Kelly smiled, but secretly she was interested in Grey's reply. She'd heard about the man who'd started a fire in the Register of Deeds Office in the Comanche County Courthouse. The fire had spread, doing major damage to the old building.

"Arson wasn't the worst of Randolph's crimes," Grey said. "He also attacked my sister, Sky, and my cousin Willow. Because of the relation, I don't feel it would be in the best interest of the people of Comanche County for me to hear the case. Therefore, I've—"

"You've removed yourself from the case and requested another judge." The senator was nodding, his expression one of respect.

Pride filled Kelly.

"That was a good call," the senator said. "It sounds to me as if there's plenty of hard evidence to put the man away for a good long time. There's no reason for you to risk involvement. Keep this up and you'll gain that position on the Oklahoma State Supreme Court I've been hearing about."

"Perhaps one day."

"The way I hear it, there's no maybe about it. Word has it you've worked for it, walked the straight and narrow. I've never heard a whisper of gossip surrounding you or your name. If there were any skeletons in your closet, they would have come out by now. You want that position, you continue to keep your nose clean."

"I didn't remove myself from that case because I was trying to win Brownie points, Senator."

Kelly couldn't have been the only one who heard the warning in Grey's voice.

Hadley Fitzgerald slapped Grey on the back. "Just one more reason why you'll make a fine addition to the state supreme court." The senator looked at Kelly next. "Some men have goals. Grey Colton has aspirations."

Kelly's smile felt stiff.

The hostess appeared. "Judge Colton? Your table is ready."

Suddenly, Kelly didn't feel so good.

Hadley and Beatrice Fitzgerald took their leave. Grey and Kelly followed the hostess to their table and took a seat. They opened their bound menus. Kelly didn't even pretend to study hers. "Would you say that appointment on the supreme court is your lifelong aspiration, Grey?''

''Hadley was being dramatic.''

Grey sensed Kelly's nervousness. Hadley and Beatrice Fitzgerald had that effect on a lot of people.

''Then you wouldn't be devastated if your career took you down a different path?''

He wanted to put her at ease, and he didn't want to talk about politics. She had a month-old baby. He understood her need to take this slow. He hadn't made reservations here with the hope of running into influential people. He'd made reservations here because the lighting was low and the atmosphere was secluded and romantic. He'd brought her here because it had occurred to him that they'd never even been on an actual date. And a woman like Kelly deserved the royal treatment. He'd brought her here because he'd never thought feeling this way about a woman would happen to him.

''You're not saying anything,'' she said.

He looked into her eyes. She was right. There were so many things he wanted to say but hadn't. Suddenly, he didn't know where to begin. ''You know something, Kelly?''

She shook her head, and, he thought, she had the greenest eyes.

''I have friends. One or two. I have my brothers and sister and parents. I have honorable goals. And okay, maybe you could call them aspirations. I think, no, I *believe* I can make the world a better place. I love Oklahoma. I loved growing up here. I love the law. Not because of some power trip, but because I want the law to work the way it was designed to work.''

"You want it to protect the innocent people."

"Yes."

She wiped away a tear.

Emotion welled within him, too. "Suddenly, I find myself sitting on a precipice that leads to every dream I've ever had, and everything I've ever wanted is about to come to be."

Everything he wanted and needed, he thought, this woman, her child, the position he'd worked for. It was all within his reach. For surely he wasn't imagining the love shining in Kelly's eyes.

"You probably have a good idea what I'm about to say." Grey found himself with the peculiar urge to grin. Would wonders never cease? "Women have intuitions we men can't fathom."

Kelly toyed with a strand of her hair. Any second now, she was going to swoon. She was pretty sure Grey was going to tell her he loved her. Before he did, she had to tell him the rest of her story. "Senator Fitzgerald said something tonight, Grey."

Something in the tone of her voice must have finally gotten through to him. He looked at her. "What did Senator Fitzgerald say?"

"He said it before and after he mentioned your aspirations. He mentioned skeletons in closets."

"It's just a phrase." He placed the menu on the table and looked at her.

She bit her lip. "I have one." Her voice was but a whisper.

"One what?"

"A skeleton. In that symbolic closet. It has to do with a lie of sorts. Something that could hurt you and maybe even keep you from your aspirations."

"Impossible. You would give away your last dollar to someone in need."

"Yes, but—"

"Come on, Kelly. You'd be a terrible liar."

She thought back to that time she and her sister sneaked out to that concert. *She* was the reason her parents had found out. Grey was right. People always, always saw right through her.

Grey looked smug.

Kelly whispered, "What about lies of omission?"

The only sounds were those the other diners were making, the clatter of silverware, the soft murmur of voices. "What about them?" Grey finally asked.

She leaned over the table, and in a shaky voice said, "There's something I've been trying to tell you for a week now. It's about Frank."

"What about him?"

"And it has to do with Alisha."

He, too, leaned closer. "I thought you said he isn't in the picture."

"He isn't."

"I don't understand."

She thought about all the ways she'd practiced saying this. She ended up looking directly at him and whispering, "He doesn't know about her, Grey."

His eyes narrowed. The expression that settled across his features reminded her of how he looked in court: quiet, assessing, in complete command and ready to make a decision at a moment's notice. He really was a brilliant man, able to think quickly and concisely. "He doesn't know you've had her yet?"

"It's more than that. He doesn't know about her. Period. I never told him I was pregnant." She let that soak in for a few heartbeats, then continued. "At first,

I didn't tell anyone. I couldn't believe I was expecting a baby. I grappled with so many decisions. Finally, I knew I had to tell him. I was three months along by then. The first time I called, I left a message on his machine asking him to give me a call back. He never did. I waited a month, then tried again. That time, a woman answered. I could tell from the sounds in the background that they were having their own private little party, and it just made me sick all over again."

Grey relaxed, and Kelly began to feel better. It reminded her that underneath his stern attitude, he was an understanding man.

"I told the woman not to bother Frankie, and I hung up. The more I thought about it, the more justified I felt in not telling him. Frankie once said he didn't want children. Ever. Obviously, he hadn't changed. And I didn't see how it could hurt any of us if I raised my baby alone."

Grey reached across the table, touching her hand with his long, blunt-tipped fingers. "I won't even try to counsel you from the moral side of this issue, Kelly, but from a legal standpoint, as the father, he not only has the right to know he has a child, but he has a legal obligation to her."

"You're right."

He relaxed a little more. "So, you tell him. I don't see how that could keep me from obtaining a position on the state—"

She silenced him with one sudden shake of her head. "There's more." She drew her hand from his and placed it in her lap.

"If you're going to tell me you've been arrested for a felony or are wanted by the FBI, I won't believe you."

"I haven't been arrested, Grey."

He almost smiled.

"But my husband was."

The waiter materialized like a genie from a magic lamp. "Are you and the lovely lady ready to order, Judge?"

Kelly looked up at the waiter, half wishing he was a genie and would grant her three wishes. It would take that many to work this all out. "I'm sorry," she said to the red-haired young man with the eager expression on his face. "But I'm afraid I'm not feeling well." Out of the corner of her eye, she could see the man wearing the somber expression. "I think it would be best if the judge took me home."

Chapter Ten

As if by mutual consent, Grey and Kelly endured the first portion of the ride from Roberto's in silence. He didn't know what rankled more, the fact that she'd referred to Frank DeMarco as her husband—not her ex-husband—or that she'd referred to *him* as the judge. The judge.

Grey loosened his tie, and opened the top button on his starched shirt. It didn't help. The temperature under his collar was still far too hot for the mild spring evening.

He'd had it all planned. Advance. Circle. Retreat. Advance. Circle. Advance.

He'd been seconds away from telling her he loved her, and...

And hell and damnation. How could his plans have gone so awry?

Normally, he was clearheaded. Suddenly, he couldn't think straight.

It was dark outside. Kelly was looking straight

ahead, her expression unreadable under the dim illumination of the dash lights.

Grey couldn't endure the silence another second.

"Are you telling me your *ex*-husband has done time?" he asked.

She shook her head and clutched her arms as if against a sudden chill. "No, Grey, Frankie didn't go to jail."

"Why the hell not?" He looked at her again.

She shivered. Any second now steam was going to come pouring out of his ears.

"Why not, Kelly?"

"For one thing, he had a good attorney."

Grey's sense of dread was getting worse by the second. "You represented him."

It hadn't been a question. She nodded anyway. "Wouldn't the press have a field day with that?" she asked quietly. "I can see the headlines now. Oklahoma Supreme Court candidate dating attorney who got ex-husband acquitted."

"Was he guilty?"

"Of course not!"

"Oh, that's right," he said. "What was I thinking? You never defend anyone unless you're sure they're innocent."

"That's right."

"And you've never been wrong about anybody."

"What does that have to do with anything?" she asked. "My reputation isn't at stake here. Yours is. It takes a lot less than a stained skirt or a missing secretary to ruin a public figure's reputation, Grey."

"You don't say."

Kelly refused to look at Grey. Outwardly, she shivered. She was cold on the inside, too. "Frank never should have been charged with anything in the first place.'' She took a deep breath. ''It happened after we were separated. Frankie and some friends were having a cookout. They were probably pretty noisy. A neighbor complained. A policeman came, and wrote a ticket for open burning. Somebody had taken pictures earlier, and the photograph clearly depicted a contained cooking fire, complete with skewers full of hot dogs and marshmallows. Frank liked to party, but he didn't break the law. Except for one time when he ran a red light because our dog had been hit by a car and we were rushing him to the vet, he never even speeded.''

''He sounds like a model citizen.''

Kelly could have let the sarcasm go, but Grey's knowing, judgmental attitude, oh, that was irritating. ''He was innocent, Grey.'' She had no idea why they were arguing about this. ''I shouldn't have to defend him again.''

''Meaning what?''

''Meaning,'' she said, her voice rising in volume, ''not even you can be the judge *and* the jury.''

''Oh, that's good. But of course! Sunny Suzy here is the perfect judge of character!''

''I never said I was perfect.''

He was breathing heavy, and so was she.

''Look, Grey. I'm sorry if I've spoiled your evening. I just thought you should know about my past. Senator Fitzgerald said it best, right? Keep your nose clean. You should be thanking me for telling you before anything could hurt your precious reputation or your chances to attain your, your, your aspiration!''

''Maybe I'm not the one you should be telling.''

"What do you mean?" she asked, reaching for the door handle.

"Why haven't you told this paragon of virtue he's a father? Is there more to it, Kelly?"

"Now you're questioning my motives for not telling Frankie about Alisha?"

Her door opened. She blinked against the sudden burst of light.

Grey didn't so much as bat an eye. "You said it, not me."

She got out of his vehicle. Lifting her chin a full three inches, she said, "I hope you're very happy someday when you're appointed to the state supreme court."

"Where are you going?"

She sniffled. "I'm going on with the rest of my life, something I should have done a month ago. I'll leave you with one last bit of advice. Throw away that Hawaiian-print shirt I gave you. You're far better suited to black and white. Oh. And one more thing. I've fallen in love with you. You're right. Turns out I am a lousy judge of character."

She was crying when she entered her house. Grey was left sitting in the dark, his heart beating an ominous rhythm, wondering what the hell had gone wrong. Kelly was the one with the doozy of a lie of omission. And yet he felt as if he had just committed a monumental crime.

"The prospective jurors are beginning to trickle in, Judge. Judge? Judge Colton?"

Grey turned his head. "There's nothing wrong with my hearing." Norma, the friendly, matronly court clerk, held her tongue until after she'd counted to ten

under her breath. "That's good to know. Do you want
to continue even though the lights keep flashing?"

"We'll wait a few minutes for the power to stabi-
lize. If it doesn't, there are windows in the courtroom.
We can't let a little thing like an interrupted power
supply get in the way of justice." He added "damn
it" under his breath.

For a man who didn't swear, he'd been saying
"damn" a lot lately. Among other things. His mother
had threatened to wash his mouth out with soap, and
she didn't care if he was thirty-three years old. The
court clerk and bailiff wanted to do more than that.

So he was a tad grouchy. So what?

It had been two days since Kelly had let him have
it with both barrels. She wasn't answering her phone
or returning his calls. He wouldn't know what to say
if she did.

He had good reason to be grouchy. He hadn't slept.
And he'd come to a blinding, screeching stop on the
road to his future. His great-grandfather called it a
fork in the road. The path leading to Kelly and Alisha
had been sealed with a mile-high brick wall. Grey
knew it was brick because he'd crashed headlong into
it more than once.

The other path was wide open, the view crystal
clear. If he chose to walk it, it would be a relatively
smooth journey to the state supreme court. The only
problem with that path was that it was so narrow he
would have to walk it alone. Alone. He ached as
much from that word as he did from body slamming
that brick wall.

He peered around him, suddenly aware of his surroundings. Norma was talking to Albert Redhawk, the
custodian. Grey's cousin, Sheriff Bram Colton, was

talking to the prosecuting attorney. Potential jurors were starting to straggle in. The man on trial had been duly cleaned up and properly dressed in order to make a good first impression. Now it was up to the justice system to see that he had a fair trial.

In Comanche County, Grey sat at the head of that justice system. It was up to him to see that the jurors were chosen honestly, and that the attorneys followed the rules as established by the law. It was an important job. He liked what he did. Sure, he had higher aspirations. That didn't mean he wasn't committed to what he did. He'd been thinking about that lately. If he never gained a higher position, would he care? Would his life have meaning regardless? What gave life meaning anyway?

The lights came on—those attached to the electrical current Albert had just fixed, and the figurative one over Grey's head. The future looked bleak no matter what position he held. Without Kelly and Alisha, he might as well go home.

Suddenly, he knew what he had to do.

It was nearly two hours before he was able to do what he had to do. The rest of the potential jurors had entered, noisily taking their seats. Grey couldn't leave. As judge of Comanche County, he took his duties seriously. He pounded his gavel, calling for order. He instructed the attorneys to get organized. Lots were cast, jurors interviewed, some selected, others released. Grey kept the dribble and dither to a minimum. The selection was accomplished in record time. A trial date was set, the jurors instructed to appear the following morning at eight o'clock sharp.

Grey shot out of the courtroom, emerging from his

chambers via the outer door before his robe hit the floor. The law was important. Now, for the most important thing of all.

Kelly's car wasn't parked in her driveway when Grey pulled his Expedition to a stop. That didn't keep him from pounding on her door. He could hear Alisha crying—music to his ears. The next time he knocked it was with less desperation but no less force.

The door opened. Instead of coming face-to-face with the woman he loved, he came face-to-face with Clara Jones, the mother of the boy Kelly had defended weeks ago. "Where's Kelly?"

"She's not here," Clara said, patting Alisha's back.

Grey could see that. Clara Jones wasn't much older than Grey. She'd raised an eighteen-year-old son by herself. Kelly trusted her. And Grey respected that trust. He motioned to Alisha. "Has she been crying like this for long?"

Clara nodded. "Babies can sense things, you know." She looked him up and down with eyes that were blue and capable of great feeling and expression. "You might as well come in."

Grey hadn't realized he'd been holding his breath until it rushed out of him with enough force to draw Clara's attention again. He felt like the kid caught dipping a girl's pigtails in the inkwell. Which was strange, because he'd never been in trouble in school. "Where is Kelly?" he asked.

Clara offered Alisha her pacifier. "She went to Tulsa."

"Tulsa? Isn't that where her ex-husband lives?"

Clara nodded. And Grey acknowledged that this was what he'd been afraid of. She'd gone to see Frank

DeMarco, a man who could turn heads with his smile alone, a man she'd shared a portion of her life with. They'd had a dog together, for crying out loud.

And they had a child.

Alisha spit out her pacifier and immediately started to fuss. "Here. Let me try." Grey took the baby into his big hands, lifting her above his head slightly so that she could look down at him. "Now, you don't really want to fuss. You just think you do."

She stopped complaining and stared at him.

"There, see?" he said. "You don't want to bite anybody's head off. Other people don't understand that, do they?"

Clara had gone out to the kitchen. Grey could hear her from here, rattling pans and glasses. He lowered Alisha a few inches. "Now what do you say you stop all this fussing? We could take in a fight. Or maybe there's a soap on TV. You choose."

The baby's mouth opened, her eyes widening in approval.

"The fight, huh?"

Her eyes crinkled, her arms and legs stiffened and her back arched, all her attention focused on Grey. She made an adorable little sound, like a screech of pleasure. And then, as if it took every ounce of concentration and energy, her entire face lit up with her smile. The air rushed out of Grey's lungs all over again.

He wanted to be this beautiful child's father. It was what he'd wanted since the moment he'd delivered her. And Kelly was in Tulsa this very moment, telling another man, a man she'd once loved, that he, Frank DeMarco, had a baby named Alisha Grace.

Grey had no one to blame but himself.

* * *

"Well, Kels-bells, if you aren't a sight for sore eyes."

"How have you been, Frankie?" Kelly dodged Frankie's smooth advance, but just barely. The man always had been half octopus. "Frank, I came to talk."

"You always were a talker, and I was always more for not talking."

"Yes, I know."

Frankie DeMarco was wearing scuffed work boots and faded jeans that molded to a backside that should have been outlawed. He still had hair five shades of brown. Although he had squint lines beside his eyes, his face was no less handsome than it had been the last time she'd seen him. He would undoubtedly be one of those men that exuded sex appeal well into their eighties.

"So what do you think of the place?" he asked.

It had taken some doing, but she'd finally caught up with him in the back storage room of a bar he'd purchased in downtown Tulsa. Personally, Kelly didn't think that owning a bar was such a good idea for a man like Frankie, but that wasn't what she'd come here to say. "Owning your own business sounds so mature," she said.

He placed a finger over his lips. "Don't tell anybody. For all intents and purposes, I'm still the goodtime guy. It's good to see you, Kels. But you can see that for yourself."

She smiled in spite of herself. "Now that you mention it."

"I'd rather show you."

Lord, had she really once fallen for that line? "I came to talk, and that's all."

He looked her up and down and back up again. As

if realizing she wasn't here to party, he turned back to the crates he was unloading. ''Did you have a boob job?'' he asked.

Kelly knew Frankie was like this. She was still shocked. ''Of course not.''

He reached into his pocket, extracted a knife and proceeded to cut through the flap of the top carton. ''Well, you're certainly lookin' good. I never had the chance to say goodbye last time you were in town.''

''The last time I was in town,'' she said, leaning a hip against the brick wall, ''you were busy dodging flying glass objects.''

He hefted the box off the top of the stack then turned to face her, his burgundy T-shirt pulling tight across his chest, his eyes glinting with mischief. ''Yeah, well, Deirdre was pretty upset about finding you in our bed.''

''How is Deirdre?'' Kelly asked.

''She's fine. I hear she's fine.'' Which meant he hadn't seen her in a while. ''She wanted to get married. It's like I told her. If *Kelly* couldn't make it work, she sure as shootin' wouldn't be able to.''

Kelly crossed her arms and shook her head, but she didn't bother to tell Frankie that *he* had to want something to work, too. She could hear construction workers out in the main part of the tavern. Before one of them barged back here, she said, ''Frankie, about the last time I saw you…''

''Don't think I don't remember that night. Nobody else is like you. Are you sure you don't want to relocate to Tulsa?'' He carted the carton to a counter near her. Instead of reaching for the contents, he reached a hand to her hair.

''I had a baby a month ago, Frank.''

His sandy-colored eyebrows shot up, and his hand

fell away from her hair. She could see the calculations taking place behind his eyes. And then shutters came down and the teasing glint was back. He returned to the stack of cartons. "A baby, huh? I didn't know you were seeing someone."

"I wasn't. Do the math, Frankie."

"You aren't going to try to pin it on me." He spoke without looking up. "We signed those papers nine months ago. If the kid's a month old, it doesn't add up to me."

"Are you denying paternity?"

He looked up at her, his eyes clear and steady. And then he used his most tried-and-true beguiling grin. "I'd make a lousy father, Kels. Hell, I still need mothering. It's what women find so appealing about me. I'm the good-time guy. Buying this business is about as mature as I care to get."

Kelly took a shuddering breath. Frankie DeMarco knew she never lied, therefore he had to know the baby was his. He was almost thirty years old, but he was right. He was the good-time guy. Six years ago, she'd found that terribly attractive. Now she thought it was sad. Drawing herself to her full height, she strode to the doorway where she'd stashed her briefcase. She unzipped it and drew out a sheet of paper. She handed it to Frank. He took it, read it, then asked for a pen.

Calling two of the construction crew into the room as witnesses, she pointed to the place each of them could sign. Just like that it was over. Alisha was all hers. Morally, she had been since the beginning. Now she was all hers legally, too.

Frankie and the younger of the other two men started talking about a new nightclub opening soon.

Kelly recapped her pen, tucked the signed form back inside her briefcase and started for the door.

Frankie and his friend were whooping it up. The sound of their laughter followed her all the way to the sidewalk out front. This was it. She was never going to see Frankie again. She blinked against the blinding sunshine. Surprisingly, she shed no tears. Or perhaps that wasn't so surprising. Frankie DeMarco was out of her life now, once and for all. He was out of Alisha's life, too.

Clutching her briefcase in front of her, she started toward her car. A weight had been lifted. As she backed from her parking space and headed for Black Arrow, she thought, *He didn't even ask if the baby was a boy or a girl.*

It was hard to believe she'd ever thought she was in love with him. She was over him now. She wondered how long it would take her to get over Grey. A year? Ten? Fifty?

She would start getting over him as soon as she got home.

Kelly spent the remainder of the trip back to Black Arrow planning her and Alisha's future and counting all her blessings. She would get over Grey. And she had Alisha. She would get over Grey. And she had her work. She would get over Grey, and she had her friends, her family, her work, her home. Thank God she had Alisha. Maybe she would get a dog. Or a cat. Which would Alisha prefer? She would get over Grey, she said to herself as she pulled into her driveway.

She would get over Grey, but apparently not yet, because he was waiting for her on her tiny front porch.

Chapter Eleven

A hundred thoughts raced through Kelly's mind at the sight of the man sitting on the top step, her daughter apparently sleeping in the crook of his right arm. The strongest was how good Alisha looked in his arms.

She parked behind his vehicle and got out. He stayed exactly where he was, watching her.

A hundred things she could have said, and out slipped, "Nice shirt."

He looked down at himself, shrugged. "I was told to get rid of it because it doesn't suit me. Apparently I used to be close-minded."

"Oh, Grey."

"There you go again, saying my name in a way that fuels my imagination."

There he went again, weakening her knees. "Where's Clara?"

"I sent her home."

"And she went?" Kelly asked.

He held her gaze and he almost smiled. "I tried threatening her. When that didn't work, I bribed her."

Kelly almost smiled, too. "With what?"

"I offered her a job. Did you know she's studying to be a court stenographer?"

Yes, Kelly had known that.

"Not that it did much good to send her home. You didn't tell me she and Brian live next door. She's been watching me out her window all evening."

Kelly glanced over, and waved at her next-door neighbor. It was nearly seven o'clock. She'd been driving for hours. It had been a very emotion-filled day. She needed to sit down. She needed to hold her child.

She needed to see Grey smile one more time.

The collar of that silly gaudy shirt fluttered in the breeze. There was nothing silly about the expression in Grey's brown eyes as he said, "Did you tell him?"

"He doesn't want her." The words came out sounding thick.

"I want her."

"Grey."

"And I want you."

She must have walked closer, although she didn't recall doing so. She would never forget the way he stood, and slowly descended the steps. "I love you, Kelly."

Tears blurred her vision.

"Will you marry me?" he asked.

"Are you crazy?"

His eyes narrowed, and he advanced, a determined look on his face. "I'm not crazy, Kelly. I'm lost."

"I don't understand."

"I took a wrong turn somewhere. My great-grandfather foretold it a month ago. I took a wrong turn. Now I'm lost. Without you.''

He stopped a foot away. The sun had begun its downward slide in the west, throwing their shadows onto the ground on the other side. ''You said you love me, Kelly. There's no taking it back.''

She smiled, because that just sounded so *boyish*. Something told her that if he wouldn't have been so focused on his future, he would have been a hellion as a child. Which reminded her…

''That skeleton in my closet isn't going to go away, Grey.''

''I don't care.'' His voice was deep, the expression in his eyes deeper yet. ''I've been doing a lot of thinking out here. Alisha isn't a lot of company when she's sleeping.''

Kelly smiled.

''I'm not complaining. I love her. She's the most amazing little kid. Care to hear what I've been thinking about?''

She doubted she had a choice, but really, there wasn't anything in the world she would rather hear. ''What have you been thinking about, Grey?''

''Your smile.''

''My what?''

''I'm drawn to your sunny smiles. I've spent more hours than I care to admit this past month thinking about your smile, wanting you, aching. You're five feet six inches tall, a very nice five feet six inches, at that. You have auburn hair, a narrow nose, a stubborn chin, legs to die for, breasts to ache for and a voice that calls to mind babbling brooks and gentle summer breezes.''

He moved to sit down, and motioned for her to join him.

"For a judge, you're very poetic." She sat next to him, her elbow touching his arm.

"I'm not finished."

She didn't bother trying to conceal the roll of her eyes.

"I even thought about you when I was hearing a case. That never happened to me before. And that was when it dawned on me. It wasn't your hair or your legs or your breasts that made you so special. It's the way you make me think, the way you make me feel, the way you soften when I take you in my arms. It's heaven. And it isn't."

"I know what you mean, Grey." She looked up at him, and very nearly drowned in his eyes.

"I believe you do, Kelly. You accepted me. Without judgment. I know, I know. I was judgmental enough for the both of us. Despite that, you offered me your friendship. I want a hell of a lot more."

"What about the state supreme court?" she whispered. "I thought that was your dream."

"Dreams change. It's true it used to be my life's purpose."

"Used to be?" she asked.

He nodded. Birds twittered. A car drove slowly by. Kelly and Grey were too wrapped up in each other to pay the rest of the world much attention.

"And now?" she asked.

"I guess it's like Clara said. Some people's life purpose is simply to serve as a warning to others."

He talked to Clara about this? Kelly's first thought. Her second was more serious in nature. "I don't want to be the reason you didn't get that position, Grey."

"Then be the reason I get up every morning, come home every night, the reason I'm happy, the reason I'm here, in this world, in this life."

It was a good thing Kelly was sitting down, because her legs never would have held her if she'd been standing. "It's a very tempting offer."

Any other man would have said something flip. Grey wasn't any other man. He was the youngest judge in the history of Comanche County. He was the man she loved. "All right," she said.

She sensed, saw, felt his surprise. "All right? That's it?"

She nodded. "I was thinking about getting Alisha a dog or cat when she's a little older."

"I don't see what that has to do with…"

"Do you think your sister would like to be Alisha's godmother?"

"Sky?"

"Do you have another sister I don't know about? And I was thinking about asking my brother-in-law to be her godfather."

"It sounds as if you've been making a lot of plans." Grey had been making plans for weeks. Circle, advance, retreat. He'd had the advantage, planning his strategy. He eased Alisha out of his arms, and into Kelly's, then held his arms out, hands made into loose fists, wrists close together.

"What are you doing?" she said, cradling her baby in her arms.

"I surrender. If you want your brother-in-law to be Alisha's godfather instead of me, so be it."

She placed a hand on his face, turning him toward her. "I have a more important, vital position in mind for you. I would like you to be her father."

Grey had been called *Your Honor* countless times. He'd never felt more honored in his life. He leaned closer, and said, "I'll take that as a yes."

"What was the question?" she asked.

"I asked you to marry me five minutes ago."

"Oh."

He cocked one eyebrow, waiting.

"If you're sure you can live without that position on the state supreme court, then yes. This is definitely a yes."

He made a sound deep in his throat, like a low growl of a wolf, and hugged her gently, reverently. "I can live without a lot of things. I don't want to live without the two of you."

"I love you, Grey."

He breathed easy for the first time in two days. Grey knew a contentment he'd never known, for he'd added a fourth and final maneuver to his strategy. Advance, circle, retreat. And surrender.

He couldn't seem to get close enough to Kelly. All the hugging and kissing woke up Alisha. As long as she was awake, she wanted to eat. Her cries rang out through the quiet neighborhood.

Kelly and Grey had a wedding to plan, and a christening, and the rest of their lives to chart. First, they had a daughter to feed. They rushed inside, and the gray wolf was lost no longer.

Epilogue

Grey and Kelly's wedding day had dawned cloudy, breezy and balmy. On this afternoon in early June, the small chapel was filled with family and friends who had come from far and near. Everyone was sure it would rain.

Grey didn't care. All the sunshine he ever needed was glowing in Kelly's eyes, made even brighter by the remnants of the tears that had coursed down her face as they'd said their vows. She was wearing a suit the color of ivory, and a hat with netting that somehow made her eyes look even more green. Surely there had never been a more beautiful bride.

Bram served as Grey's best man. Kelly's sister, Mariah, wearing a hot-pink dress and stiletto heels stood behind Kelly. There were no SWAT teams at this wedding, although Mariah's son, Lance, and Jared and Kerry's little girl, Peggy, had caused nearly as much calamity when they'd refused to walk down the aisle as flower girl and ring bearer. It had taken a total of five Coltons to convince them, okay, bribe them to carry the pillow and little basket to the front of the chapel.

Randy and Lucy Colton had flown in from Washington, D.C., their infant son, born last Christmas, quietly sucking his thumb.

Alisha was wide awake, perched on her daddy's arm, looking out at the guests. She couldn't have known that Joe and Meredith Colton had come all the way from California not only to attend this wedding, but because Joe Colton had once been a senator and was still a very influential man in the political arena. Just yesterday he'd met with a good friend of his who happened to be an Oklahoma State Supreme Court justice. Alisha's new daddy had earned the position. If he wanted it, it was going to be his.

Right now, Grey had everything he wanted. Any second now the pastor was going to pronounce him and Kelly husband and wife. Alisha's adoption proceedings were under way. His parents were sitting in the front pew, fingers entwined, gazing lovingly at each other, certainly thanks in part, to their new mission.

George WhiteBear presided over the ceremony from the back of the church where he stood dressed in the Native American attire reserved for sacred ceremonies. The gray coyote had appeared for but a moment yesterday. So many of the coyote's prophecies had come to pass. There sat Jared and his new wife, Kerry, Willow and her husband, Tyler. In another pew were Jesse and Samantha, Sky and her fiancé, Dominic. Bad Boy Billy was here with Eva. Bram and Jenna were expecting. The babies had already started to come; the Coltons had always been a fertile lot.

George's wrinkled face crinkled into a proud, know-ing smile as he gazed at the fruit of his long life.

Not everyone here had found their soul mate. His four great-grandsons, Ashe and Logan, Shane and Seth sat together, alone. The next time the coyote appeared, George would ask about them. But now, the pastor was nearly finished. Soon, this ceremony would be over, and little Alisha's christening would begin.

Kelly looked up at her husband, and smiled through her tears. The vows had been beautiful and meaning-ful, but it was saying them to Grey, who was patting Alisha's back, the ring she'd just placed on his finger glinting in the glow of candlelight, that filled her heart to bursting.

He was handsome in his black suit, black tie, his dark eyes brimming with warmth and quiet emotion. Alisha looked incredibly tiny in the gown that had been lovingly sewn years ago by Grey's grandmother, Gloria WhiteBear Colton, for each of her grandchil-dren to wear at their christenings.

Thunder rumbled in the distance. The threat of rain seemed fitting somehow. Perhaps it was because it had been a storm that had brought her and Grey to-gether. She planned to spend the rest of her life being thankful.

"You may kiss your bride," the pastor said.

Grey covered her lips with his, their daughter be-tween them. Thunder rumbled, their guests clapped, and the rest of her life with Grey and Alisha, and their future children, began.

*   *   *   *   *

Silhouette Romance presents tales of
enchanted love and things beyond explanation
in the heartwarming series

Soulmates

Couples destined for each other are brought
together by the powerful magic of love....

Broken hearts are healed
WITH ONE TOUCH
by Karen Rose Smith (on sale January 2003)

Love comes full circle when
CUPID JONES GETS MARRIED
by DeAnna Talcott (on sale February 2003)

Soulmates

Some things are meant to be....

*Available at
your favorite retail outlet.*

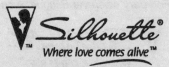

Silhouette Books

is delighted to present
two powerful men, each of whom is
used to having everything

On His Terms

Robert Duncan in
LOVING EVANGELINE
by *New York Times* bestselling author
Linda Howard

and

Dr. Luke Trahern in
ONE MORE CHANCE
an original story by
Allison Leigh

Available this February wherever Silhouette books are sold.

Where love comes alive™

PSOHT

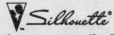

$ Saving Money $
Has Never Been
This Easy!

Just fill out and send in this form from any
October, November and December 2002 books
and we will send you a coupon booklet worth a
total savings of $20.00 off future purchases of
Harlequin and Silhouette books in 2003.

Yes! It's that easy!

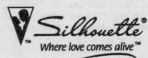

HARLEQUIN®
Makes any time special ®

Silhouette ®
Where love comes alive ™

© 2002 Harlequin Enterprises Limited   PHQ402

SILHOUETTE *Romance*

COMING NEXT MONTH